Feather
for
Forever

Alaska

Marianne Schlegelmilch

One of America's Most Gifted Writers

PO Box 221974 Anchorage, Alaska 99522-1974

books@publicationconsultants.com—www.publicationconsultants.com

ISBN 978-1-59433-648-5
eBook ISBN 978-1-59433-649-2
Library of Congress Catalog Card Number: 2016944909

Cover Art by Barb Montpas Sirmeyer

Copyright 2016 Marianne Schlegelmilch
—First Edition—

Manufactured in the United States of America.

Dedication

*To all the moms, the '65 Flint St. Agnes Crusaders,
and my loyal peeps*

~ This feather's for you ~

Contents

Chapter One

On The Beach

Mara's feet slipped on the tangled heap of slimy kelp and boulders the sea had piled around the boardwalk supports, but she managed to stay upright. Considering the size of the waves pounding the nearby sandbars, this tide was coming in with more vengeance than usual.

She zipped her sweater jacket up tightly against her throat as gale-driven sand pelted her like a blast of stinging nettles, but the measure did little to stop her shivering. Why hadn't she had the sense to bring a hat, or a headband to stop her hair from whipping across her face, and some sunglasses to protect her burning eyes? As if she had never spent time in wild Alaska before!

Waiting here, beneath the boardwalk shops that lined the Homer spit might not have been the best choice, but with all the elements working against her, she had sought the stability of anything that wasn't at the mercy of the wind or part of the raging sea as she tried to retrieve her dog and come in off the beach.

Where was Thor, anyway?

She pushed her unruly mane back for the umpteenth time just long enough to catch a glimpse of him chasing billows of sea foam across the beach.

"Thor! Come!"

As the water swooshed around her feet and slowly rose up her ankles, she wrapped both arms around one of the pilings that had once been a massive tree in some Alaskan forest. If she had even considered that her precarious position had left her vulnerable to becoming another statistic in the 15- to 20- foot tides the area was known for, she showed no evidence of it.

"Thor! Let's go! Move it!"

Darn it anyway! He seemed not to hear her as he threw himself into his game of chasing the sea foam. It was as if the storm energized him instead of driving him with her to shelter.

"Thor! You heard me! Let's go!"

She took a step sideways, slipped enough to fear she could sprain an ankle—or worse—then cautiously stepped again. Just when it seemed she had gained secure footing, her boot slipped off one of the rocks and got tangled in a loop of rope that was sticking up in the kelp.

With one arm awkwardly extended in an effort to maintain balance, she tightened her grip on the piling with the other and inched down the support to try to unloop the rope from around her boot. When it finally came loose, she tossed it away, but the water just washed it back again. How long would she be able to withstand the wind, the rain, the slippery rocks, and still fight with this rope using a hand numb from the cold?

"Thor! Go get Doug! Thor! THOR!"

At long last Thor ran to her, stopping abruptly to investigate something about three feet from where she stood. Straining against the elements, she struggled to see what he was pawing at. It looked like a human hand. Was this some kind of prank or what? She wiped her eyes with the back of her hand and looked again. It was definitely a hand! Not only was it a hand, but it was still connected to an arm.

"Thor! Let it go!" she yelled.

Her dog backed off just as the next wave crashed and rolled out, revealing not only a human arm and hand, but an entire body.

This time she screamed—spontaneously and loudly, and in a way that sounded distant and foreign to her own ears. Her obvious distress caught the attention of some surfers, who were also clambering in ahead of the tide. In slow motion, she watched two of them approach, check the situation out, and then drag the dead man out of the water and up onto the rocks, while a third guy scrambled up the beach with two dogs in tow.

"Call 911!" he yelled back as he pushed the dogs into a truck.

The shivering was uncontrollable now. Whether it was from the cold or from the sight of the body splayed less than a few feet away, she was shaking. It was fully clothed and of a young man who couldn't have been any more than eighteen or twenty. She fought back nausea. Although it looked like he hadn't been dead for long, she knew that he was—dead.

She screamed again, the sound piercing the hypnotic cadence of the waves as she continued to cling to the piling with one hand, while grabbing her cell phone with the other.

With her fingers no more than frozen nubs and her body shaking with a renewed surge of adrenaline, somehow she pushed 911 and in stuttering chatter gave dispatch directions to the site of the grisly discovery.

When she looked up, one of the surfers had returned and was staring at the body.

"Doesn't look like he's been in the water that long, but that rope around his ankles sure says that someone wanted him to be."

Mara huddled even more tightly against the piling as the cold remnants of melting snow dripped through the boardwalk slats onto her head. Through the cracks between the planks she could see boarded-up shops silhouetted against the crisp blue sky. The sun was so bright. It was weird to see it like this in the midst of such a terrible storm. It blinded her as it moved low across the horizon, so she looked back down and clung to the piling.

"Can you help me get out of here?" she called to the surfer.

Another crescendo of shivers wracked her body as she clung to the pole, while the wailing of sirens drawing closer wracked her mind.

"Grab on," he said, as if just noticing her distress.

Reaching out to him with one quivering arm, she gingerly navigated the slippery kelp until he was able to grasp her arm tightly and tug her onto the safe footing of the hard-packed sand. Once safe, she clung to him, as if letting go would send her tumbling with the torrent of rolling stones each wave carried across the black sand back into the sea.

"Thank you."

"Wait there. Till the cops come. It's got heat," he said, pointing to a beater Subaru parked next to the truck that held the dogs.

She held Thor back from trying to wiggle himself between the rescuer and herself until the surfer extended his hand for the dog to sniff, and Thor settled down.

"I'm okay, bud," she told him, as she grabbed onto his collar and walked him to the car.

She cradled his sopping wet body, gently stroking his wet fur while she sat waiting with her feet sideways out the door. In spite of being drenched, he felt warm and comforting.

What kind of welcome back to Homer was this? She and Doug had barely finished unpacking and setting up their new home along the slough. Winter was supposed to have afforded them both privacy and time, not this. Their two seiners had just arrived from Juneau last week and they had already started readying them for fishing season.

She brushed away an unexpected flow of tears.

Cold, wet, and with her emotions all over the place, she pulled her sweater jacket more tightly around her as she and Thor waited in the warm shelter of a stranger's car. The wolf dog, who had been with her through more trauma than she cared to remember, leaned into her protectively as she forced her thoughts to be anything but about the right here and the right now.

Leaning back against the seat and closing her eyes, she let a slideshow of all the happy summers she had known here on the Homer Spit play out in her head. Just as in years past, this quiet place would soon be bustling with tourists and these boarded-up shops open for business.

The scene played out so vividly in her mind. Throngs of both local and world travelers would soon be enjoying the natural beauty of this place dubbed The Cosmic Hamlet by the Sea. She could almost feel the sun on her back and hear the sounds of people, cars, boats, bicycles, and RVs roaming about.

Thor's low growl jolted her back to the reality of the raging storm and the sight of the spit still entrenched in its winter's sleep.

"Quiet," she shushed him, as she watch a police officer, who had stopped to inspect the body.

Where was the feather Joe Michael had given her so long ago? It was supposed to be here, in her pocket when she needed it. She checked the other pocket and the two in her jeans before remembering he had taken it from her to take to the totem-raising ceremony in Sitka next week.

"Needs to be refreshed," he had said.

Instead of the feather, she found one of the shells she had picked up earlier on the beach, hidden there with a mitten over it so Thor couldn't find it. Sure enough, as the mitten fell to the sand, he stood and shoved his nose into her pocket like he always did.

"Get out of there," she said, pushing him away, but he knew and she knew she didn't mean it, and so he pushed his nose around inside her pocket some more before sitting in his best good-dog pose to see if she would give him one of the special treasures to play with.

"Down, bud."

Even as he obeyed, he kept his ears perked as his eyes darted around in search of any threat despite his inclination to let his puppy self prevail.

She pulled him close again and held him, closing her eyes to shut out the reality of the scene around her. This time he didn't try to wiggle away. Instead, he leaned his body into hers as if to hold her just as he had always done since they first met—what was it, five years or so ago now?

Another police car had driven down to the beach and she could hear snippets of conversation about the body. She guessed she'd better go to them. It felt more empowering than waiting for them to come to her, and right now she needed to feel some sense of control.

She stuffed the mitten back into her pocket to protect the shells. Later, she would put them inside one of the clear vases located all over her house and served as her own unique style of decoration. But before that she would put them in the boiler room until they were dried out enough for the vases. Do normal things in the normal way—soon, away from here.

She snapped a leash onto Thor's collar, then walked over to the police car and to the two officers who had responded.

"I'm Mara Williams. I found it—you know, the body."

The rest of their conversation played out as if she were watching a movie, until after about an hour they told her she could go.

She would have to call Joe and Sal in Hoonah later than planned. They would understand when she told them.

And Doug, working only a fourth of a mile or so away, was never going to believe this! Dang, how she wished he would answer his phone.

Chapter Two

No Real Surprise

A streak of low black clouds rushed across the sun and the rain began just as the police began their job of supervising the removal of the body. If it had only been the gloomy drizzle that so often blanketed Alaska's coastline, Mara would have paid it little mind, but it was a cold, wind-driven blast coming down in an intense downpour that showed no sign of letting up any time soon.

She inched her way across the Spit Road to the harbor with her windows steaming up faster than her defroster could clear them. Despite the driving rain, she rolled one of them down so she could at least see the shape of any vehicles coming toward her.

Doug and Derrk were both sopping wet and stacking the nets on the Storm Roamer when she found them. By the looks of them, they hadn't been able to make any kind of dash for their rain gear—maybe because the power block was already pulling up the nets. She stayed back, watching the dangerous operation, unsure if he even knew she was there.

She was still quivering from the whole dreadful experience, as well as from being just as cold and wet as they were, so when Doug looked up for a moment and squinted against the rain in her direction, she honked and forced a casual wave. When he didn't wave back, she drove off. He hadn't seen her and she would not endanger him by letting him see her own distress right now anyway. He would be home soon and then she would tell him.

Hours after sitting in her idling SUV along the freight road, she left the shores of Kachemak Bay and drove home. It had been peaceful there in the downpour and for a while she had lost track of time, so much so she was surprised to find Doug pacing the floor when she got home.

"They said it was you."

"Then you know about the body?" she answered.

"At first word was that it was someone from the Valley."

She watched his skin flush with red and his eyes widen as he sat, then rose from his chair.

"You didn't answer your phone," she said, as he wrapped his arms around her.

"I couldn't talk—the nets . . . Damn!"

"I know," she answered, letting the tears she had held back fall.

"You okay? I've been out looking. Couldn't find you in the storm. Didn't know what to think . . ."

He pulled her closer, as if letting her go would suck her back into the horrible scene on the beach. They had been through so much together—and apart, actually.

"It's all over town—all kinds of talk," he said, only slightly relaxing his hold.

"I'm sorry I made you worry. I was down on the freight road," she said, stepping back. "I lost track of time."

"Joey knew the guy. Derrk's son. Remember? Something about some kind of scuffle with a seasonal worker down in Dutch the other night."

"The police already took their statement. They said I could go. Look, it's not like I've never—we've never been there before," she said, but when she looked into his eyes she saw that her words had not eased the worry she had seen in them since she got home.

"Another summer, another investigation," he joked without smiling.

She simply nodded. Their life together had been nothing less than tumultuous and they were tired—not just of the certain disruption this latest catastrophe would bring into their lives, but of its being centered in the town where they would soon begin the new fishing season—a place where there hadn't been a year in recent memory when some kind of drama hadn't happened upon the arrival of the hundreds of transient workers who gathered there, and where this year's news had become way too personal.

"Are the seiners almost ready?"

"Probably need a couple of more days," Doug answered.

"I was thinking of flying over to see Joe and Sal," Mara said. "Maybe go to the totem-raising ceremony in Sitka with them. Think you can get away?"

They had been to pole-raising ceremonies before, but this one would be special because Joe Michael had done some of the carving.

"I'll make it happen," he answered.

"Then I'll start packing," she said.

"I'm guessing Derrk's gonna be as happy as we are to get out of here," Doug replied.

Chapter Three

Two Bandanas

"It was a homicide."

Mara fought the urge to roll her eyes at this pronouncement of the obvious by the boyish-looking man dressed in casual slacks and a sport coat who addressed her from behind the window at the rear of the police station.

She resisted the temptation to spurt out a snappy comment about how it wasn't like the guy tied the ropes around his own hands and feet. Instead, she looked down at the floor until she could compose herself. When had she developed this sardonic attitude anyway? She had always been known as such a sweet person. Everyone always said so.

"Is there anything else you saw or can remember?" he said.

"No. Nothing," she answered. "I was concentrating on getting my foot unstuck before the tide came in."

"If you think of anything, remember anything—even the smallest detail—please contact us."

She watched as he reached down for something behind his desk and then handed her his card.

Sgt. Justin Smith
Special Coastal Crime Investigator FBI (temporary)
Homer, Alaska
(See reverse for contact information)

"It says temporary assignment. How long are you going to be here, Sergeant Smith?"

"About a year," he answered without looking up," As part of a temporary task force on coastal community crime. Then it's back to Idaho."

"Oh," she replied.

"You're good to go," he said, finally making eye contact. "Don't worry too much about this. Just call me if there's anything else that comes to mind and let us know if you plan to leave the area."

"Okay . . ."

Apparently sensing her anxiety about his comment he added, "In case we need an additional statement or have questions, you know."

"Okay," Mara said, again.

Hopefully this drama would become a nondrama. The body had washed ashore and had been long dead by the time she found him. What else could she add to that? What Justin Smith needed to do was to find out how the body got there in the first place, and she was the last person who knew the answer to that question.

Sergeant Smith seemed like a nice enough guy for someone so young, although he came across as a little green.

"I've handled cases like this before," he said, as if sensing her skepticism about his ability to handle a murder investigation.

"Of course. I'm sorry if—well—you seem so young and all . . ."

The flicker of a smile crossed his lips as he resumed his paperwork, but not before Mara slipped quietly out the door before she could put her foot in her mouth again. Thankfully, she would be gone from here in two days and this would all be a distant memory. Why, then, couldn't she shake the feeling that today's visit would not be the end of this saga?

She sat inside her vehicle for a few minutes, just thinking.

She had long ago given up believing anything could ever be different for her or for the man who had married her twice. As much as she wished it could be so, nothing about their life together had been normal. Certainly this wasn't normal—crime, murder, bodies. Nor had all the rest—finding Brad, losing Doug, marrying Doug again. The drama surrounding all of that had definitely not been normal. And what about

Sal and Joe and the unbelievable set of circumstances surrounding their entry into her life—or was it her entry into theirs—anyway, none of that had been normal by any stretch of the imagination.

No, Mara Benson Edwards Williams Benson Williams had long ago struck the word *normal* from her vocabulary. Her life was definitely not that. Whatever the case, even though she had long ago learned to take adversity in stride, she was somewhat shaken when she had to return to the police station just a few hours later after finding a rock and a pile of broken glass inside her garage under the window.

"Weird," Sergeant Smith said.

She watched him untie the bandana from the rock, careful to use gloved hands when he did, and unfold it just enough to see the image of a smoking volcano printed on one corner.

"It's just like the other one," he said, looking astonished.

"Other one?"

"The one tied around the ankles of the victim you found," he answered. "Same gray and same orange volcano in the corner."

Chapter Four

Ambush

Doug was pounding the last nail into a board over the broken window when Mara pulled into the driveway. She watched him hitting it harder than he needed to drive it in, leaving no doubt he was as upset as she was.

"I just don't get it," he said.

She told him about Sergeant Smith and the two bandanas as he helped her lift the groceries out of the SUV.

"I'll be glad to get us out of here," he said, "It's gonna be a couple of days though."

He set the groceries on the dining room table and told her about the previous night's emergency when Derrk's son had been rushed to the hospital.

"Derrk said it was some kind of shock," Doug told her. "Ruptured appendix or something."

"Wow," Mara said.

"I guess that medevac last night was Joey. Derrk didn't want to wait for the flight out this morning, so he drove up to Anchorage last night."

"Poor Derrk," Mara said.

She turned to put the perishables into the refrigerator as Doug unpacked the bags.

"Said it was snowing hard in the pass and he had to break trail because the plows weren't out yet."

"Thank god he made it okay," she answered.

She hadn't heard the medevac fly in last night, but she had slept more soundly than usual after the exhausting drama of the day.

"Derrk's tough," Doug said, walking toward the garage. "But Joey's out for the season for sure. Be right back. There's a couple of more bags I need to grab."

Doug's spontaneous wink made Mara smile, and for the moment she was able to stop thinking about the body, the bandana, and everything but their coming trip to Juneau.

"Derrk *is* tough, my friend."

Reaching around from behind, a man pulled Doug up to gun he held in his right hand, pressing it tightly against his head. Doug caught a glimpse of a grizzly-faced stranger, before the attacker tightened his grip and started backing him out of the garage.

"Back out of here slowly and don't be stupid about it, my friend. I don't want to have to hurt your ole lady."

Doug did as instructed, slipping through the door out of the garage before Mara had time to turn around.

"Doug, did you hear me?" she called from the kitchen.

"Doug? Where'd you go now?"

She peered through the garage door just in time to see a burly man shove her husband into the passenger seat of a red truck, and then strike him alongside the head with the butt of a gun. She watched Doug slump over, unconscious as she fumbled with the door, trying to close it and lock it, but not before the stranger saw her.

"I wish you hadn't seen that, lady."

Just then a delivery truck pulled into the driveway. Upon seeing it, the masked stranger slammed his door and took off in reverse, leaving a streak of red paint alongside the box of the delivery truck as he peeled off.

"What the—" the driver yelled, jumping out of his truck.

"He's got my husband!" Mara screamed as the red pickup sped off down their street with Doug still slumped over in the passenger seat.

"Call 911!" Mara screamed. "Call 911!"

The ten minutes it took for the police to respond did nothing to stop the abduction, nor did Mara's description of the stranger, whom she described as shady-looking, burly, and wearing a gray bandana tied around his face.

"No, I couldn't read it—It was an Alaska plate—yellow . . .

"No, he's a stranger to me—to us. You have to help Doug. Help him! I can't believe this!"

"We need to get you to a secure location until we sort this out. We'll wait here while you get your things," the officer said.

Calling Thor to her, Mara snatched and grabbed everything that seemed important and threw it into a large canvas bag she often used when she was flying out for a couple of days. Minutes later she and Thor left in the police cruiser with one officer while a second stayed behind to interview the delivery truck driver. She turned to look back through the patrol car window at what moments ago had been the place she and Doug called home before sinking down into the seat and pulling Thor near.

"We don't want you to call anyone yet." the officer said as if reading her mind. "We'll need some contact information, though, then we'll be moving you to a safe location."

Mara's mind was racing. When Thor nestled his head under her arm, she pulled him even closer. None of this could be happening. She began speaking to the officer—slowly and methodically, in stark contrast to the panic she felt inside.

"Doug had just finished boarding up the window and was helping me unload groceries when it happened. Then out of nowhere—"

"I'm sorry to interrupt, Mrs. Williams, but we'll be taking a formal statement when we get to the police station. By the way, we found this in your driveway."

With one gloved hand, he held up a gray bandana with an orange erupting volcano image on the corner.

"Apparently it isn't the first one like this that's cropped up recently."

~ ~ ~

When Mara opened her eyes, she was lying on a stretcher in the hospital emergency room with a police officer standing nearby. A minute or two later, Sgt. Justin Smith walked in.

"They say you're okay, Mrs. Williams," he began. "Apparently you fainted. They're going to release you in a few minutes. Then—now don't let this frighten you—but then we're going to take you into protective custody until we can find a safe location for you while we figure this out."

Mara's eyes widened. How could this be happening?

"We've got your dog and we've got you. The deliveryman confirmed what you told us. We're aggressively searching for your husband and the man who you say abducted him. We've got no reason thus far to suspect he's anything more than missing right now. We *will* find him and we will get to the bottom of what happened here."

Mara said nothing.

"Because of what you told us about your husband being abducted, and especially about the scarf in your driveway, and the rock identical to the one found on the dead body that was thrown through your window, every road out of town is blocked. No planes are being allowed to leave and the port is in lockdown. Trust me, Mrs. Williams, whoever did this picked the wrong location to pull . . ."

Mara tried to climb down off the gurney as a nurse rushed to keep her from falling.

"Why am I here?"

"Like I said, you passed out," Justin Smith answered.

She watched him as he stepped outside to answer his phone, sitting back down to wait while he took the call. A minute later, he walked back to her, clicking off his cellphone and jabbing it into his shirt pocket as he did.

"We just got word that your husband is safe," he began. "Two of my officers intercepted the red truck out near Anchor Point and took the suspect into custody. Meanwhile, we have your husband in a secure location until we can figure out what's going on here."

"Thank god!" Mara said.

"We need to do the same for you," Sergeant Smith said.

"But, I need to see Doug—and you got the guy . . ."

"Not yet," Sergeant Smith answered. "Not until we learn more about this."

"But he didn't do anything—I didn't do anything . . ."

"Calm down, Mrs. Williams. It's for your protection—both of you. We need to figure out how to move you out of here. There's more to this than one guy abducting your husband."

"We have a plane," Mara said quietly.

"Can you fly it?" Sergeant Smith asked.

"Yes."

"Where is it?"

"On floats on Beluga Lake," she answered.

"Is there somewhere you can go that's safe?" he asked.

"Yes. We have a place in Juneau and close friends—I mean, more than that, but—anyway, they are in Hoonah or Juneau right now."

"We'll alert Juneau police that you'll be flying in by this evening," Sergeant Smith said. "But this is what I need from you . . ."

He went on to explain that the Homer Police would need her to file a flight report, a destination address, and contact information for Juneau.

"But what if they, whoever *they* are, try to follow me?" Mara asked, revealing her experience at having been followed by persons seeking to do her harm.

"The FBI is working with the FAA and local police forces on this. Basically, only law enforcement will have your actual flight plan. A fake plan will be posted publicly. We're going to need a couple of hours, though, to get officers to the bogus destination. Once they're in place, we'll let you take off and Juneau police will meet you there to get you securely to your home."

"All that?" Mara asked.

She wiped the back of her sleeve across her forehead, stood up, sat down, stood up again, then paced around the stretcher.

"Can they meet me in Hoonah instead? I think I want to go to Hoonah."

"The armed protection won't be for long," Sergeant Smith said. "I suspect that if anyone is going to try to follow you, they're going to end up walking right into the trap we are setting up at the fake location."

"And if they don't?" Mara said.

"Then we'll just play it by ear," he answered.

"And what about my husband? Why can't he come with me?"

"It's safer if you two are in separate locations for now. It's too risky to move him anyway. He took a pretty big hit on the head and he's still wobbly. We're going to set up some kind of secure communication between the two of you."

"No! I have to get to him."

"He's been checked out at the hospital, Mrs. Williams. They did a CT scan of his head and everything looked okay. He has a concussion, and that's why he shouldn't fly. Try not to worry. We have a doctor available twenty-four/seven in case anything changes, and if anything does, be assured you will be notified right away."

Sergeant Smith paused long enough to take another call before returning his attention to Mara.

"Okay, officials will clear you to land in Hoonah. Please try to trust us on this, Mrs. Williams. Hard as I know it is, please trust us."

Chapter Five

Stovepipe

Doug Williams opened his eyes, slowly lifting one hand to rub the throbbing bump on his head. He strained to focus his eyes inside the huge, dusky garage as he looked down at the grit-covered desk against the wall and the three more just like it that sat along a narrow pathway separating this quasi office area from the shop.

Hanging engines and assorted heavy-duty tools hung from brackets and beams around the giant tour bus the mechanics had just started up. He watched as they ducked under and around the bus, using head-lamps and caged light bulbs on hooks to see what they were doing, apparently unaware of his presence.

Not wanting to call attention to himself, he tried to suppress a fitful cough brought on by the fumes until, thankfully, someone finally opened the garage door and he could breathe.

A sense of wooziness threatened to drop him like a mail sack onto the dusty desk in front of him as he stood up slowly, sending a few grimy sheets of paper sailing onto the floor around him. He grabbed onto the back of the chair to steady himself. A door slammed near a larger office area behind him. Slowly he turned to see Derrk Stanley walk out of a small room, where a utility sink was all that was visible.

Derrk avoided eye contact, drew in a deep breath followed by an even deeper one, and then finally looked at Doug.

"It's my fault this happened," Derrk said to his friend. "I don't know how to tell you except to tell you if you'll let me."

"Was that the john?" Doug asked.

"Yeah. There's a light switch near the door."

Doug stumbled toward the door, groping the wall around the corner before locating the switch that lit the small bathroom. His head throbbed in the brightness and the smell of diesel would have made him sick if he had had the energy to think about the wrenching in his stomach.

Except for a recently filled soap dispenser and a fresh roll of bright white toilet tissue that stood in stark contrast to everything else, everything in the room was covered in the grimy dust of diesel repair residue. Obviously, there had been some effort to maintain cleanliness in this environment that could never really support clean. On another day, he might even have been impressed.

He stared into a porcelain bowl that was essentially the color of the dirty oil that sat in a pan on the floor outside. Maybe it was the headache that made him see an almost artistic quality to the burnished deep amber streaks that formed the pathways for the water that flushed down the sides of the toilet after each use.

The sound of his own wry chuckle startled him. The colors reminded him of the paintings done by the old masters, where layer upon layer of oil paint had been brushed onto a canvas, baked until dried, and subsequent layers applied until the desired effect was obtained. Had it been the long Alaska winter or the knot on his head that made him appreciate the potential for art in the porcelain insides of a toilet? He chuckled again until the pain in his head and the churning in his stomach made him reach for the support of the wall.

He had just finished rinsing the grit-removing soap from his hands when he turned and nearly bumped into a gray-bearded guy dressed in clean coveralls, who was carrying a bucket in one hand and a gas mask in the other.

"Sorry you had to see that," the man apologized, stripping off a rubber glove and extending his hand for a shake.

"They call me Stovepipe," he said, withdrawing his hand when Doug did not offer his back. "Guess you and your friends're gonna be my guests for a bit."

Doug continued to exit, tossing a used paper towel into the basket as Stovepipe brushed past him into the restroom.

"Might wanna step outside for a bit," Stovepipe said. "This acid's enough to kill ya."

Then, placing the gas mask over his face, he reapplied the gloves and gave the door a little shove, leaving only a small crack to let air in.

"Stovepipe isn't kidding," a guy with the name Ted embroidered onto his work shirt said. "That's pure acid he uses to clean that thing and you don't want to breathe that stuff even for an instant."

Doug stepped outside into a day so bright he had to squint. The light made his head throb more. After three tries, he managed to get his hand up high enough to shield his face from the sun. Why was he so weak? He could see Derrk and Ted sitting on a bench across the yard, so he hobbled over in time to catch the last remnants of conversation between them.

". . . Stovepipe'll tell you himself he doesn't trust doctors. 'Won't let any of 'em *practice* medicine on me!' is how he'll put it. Rigged up that piece of stovepipe to replace his artificial leg when it broke—probably over forty years ago now. Happened in the war. Nam, I guess. Anyhow, he used urethane foam and welded the stovepipe to some kind of hinge or something. Been using it that way for as long as I've known him. I don't get it. Don't ask either. Fires him up.

"He said the leg the hospital gave him lasted only five years, but the stovepipe leg has already lasted over forty years, and he expects it'll last forty more."

"And that's exactly the same way I'd tell it to ya, too," Stovepipe said, walking up to the men. "'Cause that's jest the way the story goes. It was a big metal engine that took my leg out and now it's a big piece of metal that holds it up. It's only fitting. The metal taketh and the metal giveth."

The two men sat quietly as Stovepipe chuckled in an eerie kind of way that did nothing to calm their already shaky nerves.

Chapter Six

What, but No Why

Doug was halfway across the yard when he stumbled again, this time falling against a pile of scrap wood stacked near a storage building that stood between the house and the shop.

Darn that woozy head anyway!

"Easy," Derrk said, helping his friend to an old chair that sat rusting in the yard.

Doug rubbed his aching eyes.

"I thought you were in Anchorage," he said, pulling away.

"I'm sorry, Doug. You gotta believe that," Derrk said. "All of this—I never woulda— ya know?"

Doug squinted in the bright light and stared at the person who had been his right-hand man for as many years as he could remember. He had always trusted Derrk Stanley more than just about anyone except Mara.

"There's something else," Derrk continued. "I don't even know where to start . . ."

"How about the beginning, man," Doug said. "Like how we both ended up here for starters. Wherever here is."

"It's Joey," Derrk answered. "I told you he was sick. Medevac'd."

"Yeah."

"That wasn't the real story."

"Okay. Then what *is* the real story, Derrk?"

Oblique conversation had always irritated him and he found that to be especially the case right now.

"The other day—the beach—the body . . ." Derrk stammered, rationing his words.

"Yeah," Doug said.

"Turns out it was Joey's roommate."

"Okay."

"From Dutch."

"And . . ."

"The bottom line is Joey knows who did it."

Derrk took a long, deep breath, then wiped his brow with his sleeve.

"Joey's a good kid, Doug. You gotta know that. He's my firstborn, and he's a good, decent kid—a man now, really."

"Yeah, always seemed so," Doug said without shifting his gaze.

"When Joey got here, he was quiet. Dang if I could get him to say two words to me that first day. That's not like him."

Doug nodded.

"I tried to ignore it. Figured he was tired or something, but when he came in drunk the other night I knew we had to talk. I mean, don't get me wrong, Joey's twenty-one now and he'll knock down a beer once in a while, but not to the point he's drunk. Never. Okay, maybe once or twice when he was younger, you know, with the guys, but my Joey's not a drinker."

Doug stood and stretched before sitting back down, reaching for the chair back when dizziness overcame him again. Derrk watched him, and then pulled a bottle of water out of his pocket and took a gulp.

"Want a swig?"

Doug brushed away the offer with a wave of his hand.

"It took me three days to get it out of him," Derrk continued. "Drugs. Some kinda ring. The greenhorns, they were only a front . . ."

Derrk's words trailed off as Doug became lost in his own thoughts. He knew the story without having to hear the details. Young guys recruited to run drugs to the Aleutians under the guise of being deckhands. The industry was thriving, the money lucrative. He'd known a few good guys who had fallen into the trap of big money and the rocketing need for a bigger high. Some of them were dead now.

". . . thank god," Derrk ended.

"Sorry— Say that again. My head. . ." Doug said, trying not to let Derrk know he hadn't heard every word.

"I said, thank god Joey's not mixed up in that," Derrk said. "At least he wasn't until three days ago when they ambushed Q.T."

"Q.T? Was that who Mara found on the beach?"

"Yes," Derrk said. "Joey's roommate, Q.T. And Joey knows who did it and that's why they want him now. I snuck him out two nights ago. I made up the medevac story. I needed some time to think."

"You could've come to me," Doug interrupted. "Why didn't Joey go to the police? Why didn't you?"

"I was scared they'd come after me, or worse yet, Joey," Derrk said. "The whole thing threw me. When they got you, well, that really blew my mind. Why you? Were they following me to try to find Joey? All kinds of crazy thoughts were running through my head.

"I finally did go to the police, though. I told them what Joey knew and I told them I sent him away—that he had nothing to do with it, didn't see nothing, just heard the talk is all. That's how I ended up here and then they told me they found Joey, too, and he told them everything.

"They've got him in one of those safe houses, but the gang—they don't know that."

Derrk buried his face in his hands.

"Luckily the cops got to you before they could do any real harm or hold you hostage or whatever they wanted you for," he finally said. "I was shocked to see you here—and relieved. Almost as surprised as I was to be here myself, considering they probably could have pressed charges for me helping my son—but they didn't."

The sound of Stovepipe's voice booming behind them cause both men to jump.

"Let's get back inside. Dang leg's killing me today," Stovepipe grumbled, as he hobbled past them toward the garage.

Derrk helped Doug up as the men exchanged a puzzled look.

"I know what you're wondering," Stovepipe said, turning back.

Doug and Derrk exchanged glances again. Was this guy a mind reader or something?

"You never heard of the witness protection plan?" Stovepipe barked. "Well, I'm your witness protection plan—your safe zone, or whatever you want to call it."

"Look, man, I didn't witness anything," Doug said, sounding more defiant than he looked.

Who was this guy anyway?

"Well, it's pretty obvious someone wants you here," Stovepipe answered. "Why that is I couldn't tell you, but maybe the bad guys figured you was helpin' out your friend here."

Derrk stared at the ground, silent, and not even making eye contact with Stovepipe or with Doug.

"That seems like a stretch," Doug said. "And how is it you know so danged much about it all anyway?"

"Well, Derrk's your right-hand man, and it's also no secret around here you've got plenty of money," Stovepipe said. "You can speculate all you want, or you can let the cops do their job. The bottom line is that the bump on your head should be enough to tell you that you're in danger—danger from them, whoever *they* are."

"I don't know who you are or what you want with me, but I need to get home to my wife," Doug said, getting up. "Before she gets dragged into this. They already threw a rock through our window. She'll be looking for me and don't think she probably hasn't already been to the cops."

"You're not going anywhere," Stovepipe said, turning to face Doug. "Your wife's safe. That's all I know right now, except to tell you the very cops that you keep throwing in my face have told me to keep you safe. Now why don't you just sit back down and behave yourself, because you and your friend here aren't going anywhere."

Chapter Seven

Stormy

Ted Bunson had worked for Stovepipe for the better part of ten years. During that time, he had seen the full array of mankind in the customers who visited Stovepipe's shop, but never had he seen anything like the woman with the head full of turquoise hair, who was now standing on tip toes trying to reach the platform where he was disassembling an oil-soaked part.

"I've always admired a man with a good set of tools," she said, exposing her gray roots when she pushed her hair back while speaking. "Name's Chloe Pearl Jean Maxwell, but my friends call me Stormy."

Ted acknowledged her extended hand by indicating his hands were soaked with oil.

"Pleasure, ma'am. If you're looking for Stovepipe, he should be back in a minute."

Ted slid back under the bus he had been working on, while the woman brushed diesel dirt from the blouse that barely contained her ample bosom.

"Yeah, sure," Stormy said.

She rolled her eyes as she walked away, running her hands over the jeweled dolphin on her shirt as she murmured something about Ted lacking hospitality.

"Who the hang's them two?" she said loudly, pointing at Doug and Derrk, but Ted showed no sign of having heard her.

"Never you mind about them or anyone else in my shop, Stormy," Stovepipe said as he walked in from outdoors.

"Whatsamatter, baby?" Stormy asked.

She reached down to scratch the butterfly tattooed on her ankle and then straightened her khakis, stooping to tie a bow in the ties that dangled from the pants that ended halfway down her legs.

When she stood up again, Stovepipe slid one arm around her waist and pulled her near as the two engaged in a public display of affection not often seen in their age group.

"Now, why don't you just get on home so's I can finish my work, darlin'. And while you're at it, put a coupla beers in the fridge for later, okay. Ol' Larry's feelin' a little frisky today."

Few except for Ted had ever known Stovepipe's real name of Larry Allen Kenton, and even fewer had ever heard him refer to it himself, so the fact no one but he and Stormy were now in the room pretty much confirmed the two of them were on pretty close terms.

Ted chuckled as he worked behind the bus's door. It was amazing how many facets to his persona his longtime friend had. There was no denying that this alone was the very reason why Stovepipe made such a good undercover cop, and why he insisted no one else but Ted be his partner—at least, that's the way the two had managed to work it for the past twenty-three years.

"How about you take call tonight, Ted," Stovepipe called, tossing a cell phone to his partner, who somehow caught it in midair and then stuffed it into his jacket pocket.

"Sure thing," Ted said without looking back up. "Figured that was coming."

Chapter Eight

Last One Out

The floats laid gentle ribbons across the mirrored image of leafless trees and empty cabins overlaying Beluga Lake as Mara taxied her plane toward the far shore before turning it and readying for takeoff.

She felt the Cessna lift off, first skimming the quiet water before rising above the last remnants of the night fog that had blanketed the lake. Her hands tingled from the vibration of the yoke as she clutched it with all the intensity she could muster.

Other than during training, this was the first time she had attempted a water takeoff. The remembrance of the four people who had died while landing a similar aircraft on this very lake two summers ago made her shudder even though takeoffs were known to be easier, and her own had been remarkably smooth.

She forced calmness, taking several deep breaths as she circled over the Homer Spit and then headed toward Southeast. To her left, she could see the massive Kenai Refuge wildfire burning, its acrid smoke currently moving north and away from Homer. She had been the last flight allowed to leave, and then only due to direct intervention by law enforcement officials, who had facilitated clearance in order to move her to safety. With Thor tucked safely inside his crate in the rear of the plane, she was on her way to Hoonah.

Thankfully, she had been able to talk to Doug before leaving. Law enforcement had made that happen. Although she didn't know where he was, he had convinced her that he was safe—both from the fire and from those who had abducted him.

He and Derrk had talked, he had assured her, and were back on track as both friends and coworkers.

He had then outlined his plan to—with Derrk's help— move the *Driftfeather* and the *Storm Roamer* over to Bristol Bay for the next month now that going to Juneau was out of the question. They would stop in Dutch Harbor and hire a crew from among the greenhorns assembled there, with each seiner taking on two crewmembers in addition to a third who would actually be an undercover member of law enforcement.

The adventure would be dangerous, but necessary, not only because one life had been lost already, but also because Derrk's son's life had been threatened—not to mention his own.

"We've gotta try to help," he had told her. "Better than sitting around doing nothing."

She hadn't argued except for insisting he make sure he was feeling better before leaving. Living alongside drama was nothing new to either of them at this point, and she had long ago given up trying to understand why she and Doug always seemed to be in proximity to danger. The answer remained as impossible to find as the reason they had found themselves at the core of so much turmoil.

Thor shifted inside his crate, causing the plane to shimmy ever so slightly.

"Take it easy, bud," she told him, trying her best to sound calm.

But Thor had been with her too long to not pick up on her anxiety, and so he was restless—a situation made even worse by the fact he was confined and unable to come to her rescue at a moment's notice.

By midafternoon she had re-fueled in Cordova, stopping long enough to grab a bite to eat and to let Thor have a quick run before taking off again for Hoonah. As far as she knew, no one had recognized her there, even though she and Doug had often visited the small community. If that was a sign she blended in, then what more could a person on the run hope for?

It was near midnight when she landed in Hoonah—another scary first, landing in the semi dusk of the midnight sun. After securing the plane and unloading Thor and the one bag she had managed to pack, she set out on foot for Joe and Sal's place.

With her revolver on her hip, she defied her very real fear of meeting a bear along the way. She let Thor run ahead. He was smart and on alert—better protection than the gun, actually. When she made it to the cabin, she was relieved to see a light on inside.

Through the window she could see Sal reaching into the refrigerator for a late-night snack, so she knocked gently on the door. Suddenly the old woman spun around and grabbed her shotgun.

"It's Mara," she called, stepping back from the door. "Don't shoot, Sal, it's Mara."

Chapter Nine

Déjà Vu Vu Vu Vu Vu . . .

An eerie calm fell over Mara when Sal raised only one eyebrow instead of her usual two at the news her daughter relayed.

"Look, Jane," Sal began, using the affectionate name she had long ago given to Mara. "It isn't like you haven't been here before. I mean you've become experienced at being on the run, so let's just roll with it—see where it takes us."

Sal's chuckle was followed by a nervous laugh from Mara. The two shared a long history of meeting up under extreme circumstances, long before Mara had discovered the old woman was really her birth mother, Sylvia LaMonte. Somehow, through each adventure, Sal had always come through for her when she most needed help. Although the thought did little to calm Mara's fears about the future, it did provide some small comfort that she wouldn't be facing whatever *it* was alone.

"First off, I think we should pull your plane into our shop. No sense advertising you're here," Sal said. "Then I think you should take a couple of days to see how things are gonna play out. See if anything crops up, you know? Maybe even take a little day trip or something."

Mara stared aimlessly out the window before her eyes locked on three sea kayaks leaning against a shed.

"Maybe you're right, Sal," she answered. "Have you and Joe been out in the kayaks lately?"

"C'mon, Jane. It's only April and us old folks are kinda partial to good weather. Della's been out a couple of times, though. Said she's already been seeing humpbacks out near Port Frederick."

Maybe a day trip was just what she needed.

~~~

Two days later, Mara met up with Della and some of her friends, who were heading out on a kayaking expedition to Port Frederick. Although, as Sal had pointed out, it was early, most of the members of the group were seasoned Alaskan guides who were experienced in cold-weather travel, and who were making the trip to check conditions for the upcoming tourist season.

Before leaving, the two were enjoying breakfast with Sal and Joe when Mara learned that Joe would be taking the feather with him to Sitka in a couple of weeks.

"I was hoping I could take it with me today," she said.

Joe began fidgeting with his fork, looking down at his plate and saying nothing until Sal nudged him with her elbow.

"The thing is, I put it somewhere safe. So safe I can't find it right now," he said. " Well, I got a coupla weeks . . ."

Mara furrowed her brow.

"Don't worry, dear, we'll find it in time for the ceremony," Sal said. "Now you two get on down to the beach so your group doesn't leave without you."

Chapter Ten

Calving Glacier

M ara's kayak glided seamlessly across the waters of Icy Strait. This had turned out to be a really good idea. Even when a group of Steller sea lions began following the group a bit too closely, a feeling of exhilaration displaced any of the angst she had been experiencing over the past week. Not that she was unaware of the present danger, but thankfully, she was in the middle of the group of eight kayakers and not in direct proximity to the probably 2,000-pound, 10-foot-long male that was leading a harem of smaller females behind him.

"Those people from California can't believe how big our sea lions are," Della said as she pulled her kayak up beside Mara's. "The ones down there are no bigger than seals, you know."

As suddenly as they had appeared, the sea lions were gone from sight. The answer became startlingly clear when a pod of Killer Whales surfaced about 1500 feet ahead of them. When a whale expert in the group identified them as transient orcas, the lead kayaker told the group to huddle up for safety.

"They're more aggressive," she said. "Stay tight so we look big."

As the group sat at a near standstill, huddled as tightly as they could manage, the orcas circled them several times, giving everyone a too close look at the gray V's that ringed the necks of their wet black bodies. Thankfully, after an interminably long three to four minutes, the whales moved on.

"Whew! That was close," Della said.

The first day out had certainly been an adventure!

The next couple of days were fairly uneventful—at least in comparison to the first—and it wasn't long before everyone settled into a relaxed approach to their shared adventure.

The day the group paddled up to the west arm of Glacier Bay National Park was one of the warmest and sunniest April days Mara could remember since her arrival in Alaska. As per usual, she had brought along three layers of coats, mittens, hats, and hand warmers, but for the most part, they ended up staying stashed in a waterproof bag she had tied to the back of her kayak. As tempting as it was to peel off the upper half of her dry suit, though, she resisted.

Suddenly an enormous slab of the blue ice crashed into the water about a quarter mile away, followed several seconds later by the crack of the sound wave. The swell created by the calving glacier sent the seals that had been resting on icebergs scrambling into the water and gave the kayakers a pretty wild seesaw ride as their kayaks rocked violently in the ice-filled bay.

Mara had seen glaciers calve before, but never from a kayak. She wanted to reach in her pocket for the feather, but dared not to let go of her paddle. Besides, she didn't have it anyway. Hopefully Joe had found it by now.

Another kaboom sounded after an even bigger chunk of ice crashed into the water. It had to be ten to fifteen stories tall. She wasn't good at sizing things up, but it was huge. Once the water had settled down, the group began to retreat. She would not have missed the experience–especially after feeling relief at not having died—but things were feeling a little unstable around the glacier and so it was time to go. Besides, the orcas were probably still nearby—otherwise, why were the seals back up on the ice floes?

When she finally had her feet planted solidly on the shore, she threw her head back and laughed right out loud. Here she had been worrying about a tiny little feather when she had just done something she now knew only a fool would attempt to do, and that was to kayak in an open field of sea ice, where a fall into the water would give her 3-4 minutes at most before the cold would overtake her ability to move—even with her dry suit.

Later, as she slept in one of the cabins owned by the tour group, she dreamed of Brad. Weird that she dreamed of her dead first husband. Was he visiting her? Was he watching over her? A strange mix of comfort and sadness overwhelmed her and she buried her head in her pillow until her tears made it too uncomfortable to lie on.

This whole experience, this whole presence in Alaska was because of Brad. It had been his dream, not hers to come here. Now, in this remote place near ancient glaciers, he was in her consciousness as if he were still alive. He would probably have eagerly joined the other kayakers, daredevil that he had been, but she was certain—dead certain—that he would never have allowed her out in the bay as close to a calving glacier as she had been.

Despite the strange comfort of feeling his presence, the thoughts of him scared her. Although her love for him had been real and she had believed his for her was, too, in the end he had betrayed her—or had he protected her? A look out the window at the dancing northern lights only added to her feeling of fragility.

Why did she always seem to think of Brad when the aurora was active? Was the legend about them being the souls of the departed true? She had to stop thinking about him. And what about Doug? Was he safe? Was she? It was Doug she needed to worry about, not a man who had never even been the person he claimed to be, and who was definitely, decidedly, officially dead.

A glance at her watch told her it was 3 a.m. Under the aurora she could see the glacier off in the distance. Was that a brown bear walking along the water's edge? Were they up already?

She pulled the curtain over the glass as if not seeing it would protect her. Then, for good measure, she checked to be sure the door was locked. She rifled through her duffel bag for her .45 and put it on the bedside stand, making sure it was loaded—all the while knowing that taking a bear down with such a weapon would require a lucky, well placed shot. Then and only then did she climb back into bed, burrowing beneath the comfort of a thick, down blanket before falling asleep—that is, after taking the last silly step of propping a chair against the door.

Chapter Eleven

Solitude

"You seem kinda worried," Della said as she and Mara walked to the small dining cabin for breakfast the next morning.

"I'm okay, Della," Mara lied.

"Okay, but I thought you seemed worried."

"Aunt Sal said she thought so, too," Della persisted. "She texted me this morning."

"I didn't know she could text," Mara laughed.

"Okay. I get that you don't want to talk."

Della was like that. Quiet—a woman of few words. But when she spoke, she said what was on her mind and in her heart.

"I'm sorry, Della. I just need to think."

Della winced and pulled back when Mara teasingly nudged her arm.

"Oh, gosh! I'm so sorry, Della."

Why hadn't she thought first? No way would she have intentionally pushed on the very arm that took a bullet during a robbery several years ago and left Della lying at her feet in a dark motel parking lot.

"No worries," Della said, forcing a smile. "It didn't really hurt anyway."

"I'm really sorry, Della."

"I think I'm gonna go back to Hoonah early," Della said. "There's a plane bringing supplies over and I'm gonna catch a ride with them this afternoon. Aunt Sal needs me to help Uncle Joe find the feather in time for the totem-raising ceremony. They postponed it, you know—until Uncle Joe can find the feather."

Before Mara could answer, Della was gone.

She didn't go after her. Della would be fine. She was a person who lived in the moment and took things at face value. She liked that about her. Della was real. She'd be leaving herself soon, but she wanted one more day alone before she went back to Hoonah.

Instead of going out kayaking with the group this time, she opted to stay back. Sitting on a bench outside her cabin later that afternoon, she breathed in the clean cool air. Even the fact that a bear was in the area didn't bother her now that her nighttime fears had vanished. When she saw it return and walk along the tide line with three yearling cubs, she picked up her camera instead of her gun and snapped away.

The sow kept moving, not even giving her a glance. The boom of a calving glacier, then another a few seconds later, pierced the silence. Otherwise, it was so quiet here that the gentle ripple of a breeze and the distant crackling of ice were all that could be heard.

She pushed any more thoughts of Brad out of her head and thought of Doug. Before leaving Hoonah, she had left the following text message on his phone in what she hoped would pass for some kind of code: I'M WITH MY MOM.

No one except Doug, Della, Joe, and a few officials knew about Sal being her mother, so, hopefully, once he saw the message he would call Sal and find out she was okay.

But, was *he* okay? Supposedly, he was being protected, but, still, how could she really be sure until they could talk again?

And what was with Della needing to help Joe find the feather? That didn't sound good at all.

Maybe staying back from the group had been a bad idea. Spending too much time in her own head was beginning to undo all the peace the visit to the lodge had brought her.

She made the decision then and there. She would go back tomorrow after all.

Chapter Twelve

Together again, Kind of, Sort of

When Sal told her that Doug had called yesterday and had left a number for her to reach him, she dialed it before even unpacking only to learn he was back in Homer getting ready to leave for Dutch Harbor with Derrk and Joey.

"It's not safe for me to talk on this phone, Mara. Everything I just told you is already public information. Call Justin Smith for details, but let me just say I love you, I miss you, and I'm safe. You okay?"

She told him about the kayak trip and even about the dream about Brad.

"It was intense," she said.

"It sounds like you got into some real solitude, Mara, and you got in touch with the inner you. There's nothing wrong with that. You told me something similar happened right before we met on the Alcan. Sometimes you just have to face your past head on. Alaska is the perfect place to do that."

"Did Thor get there okay? How is he? And your head?" Mara said, suddenly changing the conversation.

"He's right here," Doug said, going on to tell her that Derrk had left Juneau yesterday and stopped to pick Thor up before leaving to join him in Homer.

"I figured you'd be okay with him being on the seiner so you didn't have to worry about watching out for him. My head's fine now, too. No problems."

"Can I talk to him?"

Doug held the phone to Thor's ear as Mara talked.

"He tweaked his ears when he heard your voice," Doug said after a long pause. "He even pushed his nose onto the phone like he does when he's kissing you. Pay attention, I'm doing the same thing."

Mara laughed at the way Doug knew just what to say to calm her.

"I feel better that he's with you," she said. "I've got Sal and Joe to look after me, but you've got no one out there."

"Well—look, I can't say anymore right now, but I'm fine, okay. Just know that."

"Della said the feather's still missing," she said. "Joe's frantic. Doesn't want to go to the totem ceremony without it. Della said they post-poned the ceremony until he finds it."

"He will, and you're hanging in there just fine without that feather," Doug said. "Don't worry, it'll turn up when you need it most."

The next several minutes flew by as the two talked about everything they could think of to share.

"When I get home I'm never going to let you out of my sight again," Doug told her.

"Never?" she teased him.

"Never," he answered. "Not for any reason, any time, any place, or any anything—and you can take that to the bank."

"I love you, too," she whispered.

"I'll call you in two days," he said. "By then you'll have had time to talk to Justin Smith and get up to speed on what's going on. Meanwhile, know I love you, I've always loved you, and I always will love you. Bye, baby."

"Bye, Doug. I love you, too."

Chapter Thirteen

A Plan Sprung

S al walked into the kitchen just as Mara hung up from her call to Justin Smith. She watched the old woman put a kettle of water on the stove and then stared out the window until the person she now knew as her mother brought two cups of tea to the table by the window and sat down across from her.

"You look pretty serious," Sal said, gently pushing a cup of the hot brew in front of Mara. "I thought the kayak trip would've relaxed you."

"I just talked to the investigator," Mara answered. "Doug and Derrk are already on their way to Dutch Harbor in the seiners. Joey is with his father on the *Driftfeather*. An undercover agent named Hamlet is with Doug on the *Storm Roamer*."

"Hamlet! Now isn't that just poetic," Sal snickered.

Mara tweaked her mouth into a half smile at Sal's description.

"I don't find these people," Sal said. "They find us."

Sal always knew what to say to make her laugh.

"So what's the plan?" Sal asked.

Mara explained that according to Justin Smith, the two seiners were going to stop in Dutch as planned, load up on supplies, and hire two extra crew members, one for each boat.

"Then they're going to head to the Bering Sea and see what happens."

"That's a long ways off to be alone with a couple of crack-pots," Sal muttered.

Mara got up and took her empty cup back to the sink, keeping her back to Sal so the old woman couldn't see her fighting back tears.

"Look Mara," Sal said. "I shouldn't have said it so bluntly."

"It's okay," Mara said, breaking down into a full-blown bout of crying.

Sal walked over to her and rubbed her shoulders before heading to the living room.

"You go ahead and cry, Mara," she said. "Then pull yourself together, 'cause we're going to Dutch Harbor. It's one of the reasons I let Derrk take Thor to Doug while you were gone."

~ ~ ~

"That's right, Joey."

Sal's salty persona always seemed to surface whenever danger was near, and by the sound of her voice, she was preparing for battle.

"I understand why you can't join us, but we'll be fine."

"I got to find that danged feather," Joe muttered.

As silly as it seemed for a man well into his seventies to be this distraught about a simple feather, it had become such an integral part of his life he felt lost without it.

"You'll find it when you're supposed to," Sal answered. "There's a reason it's missing, and there's a reason ya ain't findin' it yet."

She waited for her words to sink in, staring at her husband out of the corner of her eye as she bustled about the kitchen. When she saw him settle into his recliner, she continued.

"We're gonna leave the morning after next," Sal said. "So you're gonna need to stay here to run the business. You okay with that?"

"I'm okay with it, Sylvia," Joe Michael said, letting her know with the use of her proper name that he was getting a bit peeved at her barking.

His irritation was not lost on Sal.

"I'm sorry, Joey," she said. "I guess I just slipped in to my take-charge mode what with trying to come up with a way to help Mara."

"I know , Sal," Joe Michael answered. "I'm just as worried myself, but the feather . . ."

"It'll turn up, sweet baby," Sal said. "Just try not to panic. All that's gonna do is raise your blood pressure and make it so you can't think straight. Besides, didn't we all agree it isn't the feather per se that is protecting Mara, but her own inner strength?"

"I love it when you use those big words, Sal. Parsay or what was that? That French or something? It sounds French."

"Actually, it's Latin, Joey—" Sal began, before stopping abruptly to pull some pans out of the cupboard.

"You're messing with me, Joe Michael," she laughed. "You know as well as I do what I meant and so for your trouble, well, I think maybe you're going to need to do the dishes tonight—and maybe tomorrow night, as well. Maybe even forever."

Chapter Fourteen

Text, Don't Call

S al had decided they would take the ferry to Dutch Harbor instead of flying there.

"It'll give us time to think," She said.

Mara spent the rest of the day securing the kayaks and pulling the plane into the Quonset hut at Beachmopper's Gallery, which she did with the help of Joe and his four-wheeler.

"I'll go through 'er and make sure everything's tuned up while you're gone," Joe said.

She had known he would say that even before he spoke. The old man had always been a stickler for detail. His old dualie looked brand-new even now that it was several years old. Joe was always out polishing it, fixing scratches, and detailing the custom wheels so the truck shone in the best possible way.

A phone call to Justin Smith confirmed what Doug had told her, and although he said he wasn't comfortable with Sal's plan, he didn't try to stop them.

"I'll just put a tail on you two," he said. "You'll never know he's out there. "We know you're a target," he added, "so I'll just budget it as a combination of evidence gathering and witness protection."

The serious tone of Justin Smith's voice scared Mara, but not enough to stop her from following through with her plan.

"It's good to know someone's out there watching over us," she said. "Thank you."

"One other thing, Mara," Justin Smith said. "We're going to need to start texting instead of calling or emailing. I think it's safer. I want to keep you as far under the radar of whoever these thugs are as I possibly can."

"But how?"

"I'll have someone from Juneau PD send it in an email to Beachmopper's under the subject of 'What time do you open?' It'll be signed with the name, J. D. Smith."

"Okay," Mara answered.

"Just text me when you get it and then we'll be up and running."

An hour later, the email came in and a text back assured Mara that this new communication with Sergeant Smith had been established.

"I think it's a bunch of hooey," Sal sputtered. "Like we need some cop skulking around to watch our every move."

Mara didn't respond. Maybe it was and maybe it wasn't a good idea. They had always made out all right before, but then again, there could always be the first time their luck could run out.

"I'm going for a walk," she finally said.

She took the narrow path behind the Quonset hut out toward the tall spruce stand that was part of Tongass National Forest. She had taken this path many times before when she wanted to think or just needed to be alone. Because Thor was gone, she took her .45.

The salmon weren't running yet, but bears were frequent visitors around the creek that ran behind the property and the sows would be bringing their cubs out about this time of year. There were plenty of places where matted down spots in the tall grasses meant one or more of them had recently bedded down. She was used to seeing these signs of their presence and had seldom seen the animals that had made them, but she was alone now and ran the risk of startling one, so she was careful—and a bit wary about her decision to have come here alone in the first place.

A sudden rustle in the bushes put her on alert. She moved ahead slowly, keeping her hand on the gun and being sure to make plenty of noise as she walked along, although not with her voice, in case it wasn't a bear. She could almost hear Doug asking her what she thought she was doing out here alone.

What if it hadn't been a bear?

She spun around, checking every detail of her environment. Nothing. She stood as still as a post and listened. No unusual sounds. She backed up about ten feet. No change except for the hairs on the back of her neck were standing up and giving her cold chills.

Suddenly, she saw a flash of brown out of the corner of her eye and backed up some more. She heard another rustle before she saw the cause of the disturbance. There, in a small meadow near the creek sat a sow bear basking in the sun as her two cubs scurried around her and then began to nurse.

Hopefully, they hadn't heard the loud sigh that escaped from her lips as she continued to back away. With the wind in Mara's favor, the sow continued nursing, seemingly unaware of her presence.

When she got back to the Quonset hut, she let herself in the back door and locked it.

"You okay?" Joe Michael said, looking up from where he had been working on the engine of the Cessna.

"Yes. Yes, I am," Mara said, letting out a short laugh. "Definitely."

Chapter Fifteen

That Was No Bear

"I don't like that you and Sal are taking off without the feather," Joe Michael said as Mara watched him work on the Cessna. "I feel like it'll be my fault if something happens to you."

"How can that be, Joe?" Mara asked him before giving him a hug.

She had come to love the old man, who had made it his life's mission to watch over her ever since he had watched her own father, who was his close buddy, die in the Vietnam War.

"We'll be okay, Joe. Please don't worry," she told him. "I know the feather will turn up, and I know it will happen in time for the pole-raising ceremony, so just relax—for me, okay?"

Joe Michael dabbed his eyes with the back of his hand.

Mara was as dear to him as if she were his own daughter. He would worry about her until the day he died, whether she told him to or not.

"The engine looks pretty clean," she said as she looked at the plane.

"Yeah. It's clean enough," Joe answered. "But I'll re-set the plugs and a few things just to make sure it's all tip top."

He watched Mara leave and had just picked up a wrench to work on the plane's engine when he heard something rustle outside, and then rub against the Quonset hut.

"Oh, I forgot to tell you—"

"Stay back!" Joe ordered Mara, who had come back to tell him something.

She froze in place as Joe Michael picked up his shotgun and slowly opened the back door.

"Don't shoot her," Mara begged. "She has two cubs."

Joe Michael brushed his hand back toward her as if to shush her, then slowly raised the shotgun to his shoulder from his stance inside the door frame of the Quonset hut.

He didn't call out any warning before he fired the first shot, nor did he for the next three that failed to impact anything but the stand of young spruce that had sprung up where the old wood pile used to be.

"All I saw was a glimpse of his back," Joe told her. "And by *he* I don't mean your sow bear, I mean a human being—a man dressed in a long brown coat."

Instantly—well, as instantly as she could will her fingers to move—Mara texted the info to Sergeant Smith.

Immediately he texted back: Go NOW! MY MEN WILL BE TAILING YOU BY TONIGHT. I'LL ALSO PUT SOMEONE ON JOE. MEANWHILE, TAKE SAL AND GO. TELL JOE M. TO GO TO SITKA. THEY WON'T LOOK THERE. JS

"Justin Smith wants you to go to Sitka at once," Mara told Joe. "He said it's urgent and he is putting an undercover man out to tail you."

"I really don't think I need—"

"Joe, please," Mara begged. "Please go to Sitka. This is more serious than you think. Please cooperate—for me."

Joe laid down the wrench and pulled the cover down over the engine of the Cessna.

"I'm gonna have to fly her," he said simply.

"Do what you have to do, Joe," she answered. "Justin will take care of any issues that crop up. I know he will."

"You and Sal come with me. You can catch the ferry out of Juneau."

Exactly forty-seven minutes later, they were airborne with Joe at the controls. When they got to Juneau, Joe taxied the Cessna down the runway to a relatively remote part of the fence that surrounded the airport. Handing Mara a pair of heavy wirecutters, he told her to cut a hole in a long line into the wire fencing, then push hard to bend the fence and squeeze through.

"The plane and all the dense foliage will be blocking any cameras, but you'll have to hurry as I have to make it look like the plane stalled for a moment and then keep going."

"Like I said, you'll have to move quickly. I'm only gonna slow down enough to let the two of you jump out."

"But what about you, Joey?" Sal said softly.

"Soon as I get clearance, I'll be off to Sitka."

He then pulled out the phone Mara had given him for Christmas.

"Good thing you taught me to text," he laughed. "Now what's the address for that Justin Smith fella? I'll let him know where I am and you do the same."

"I love you, Joey," Sal said.

"Be careful, Joe," Mara added.

"It's almost time," Joe warned as he brought the plane to a momentary standstill, and then revved the engine to make it look like he was recovering from a near stall.

It all happened in enough time for Sal and Mara to leave the plane and cut the wire as Joe had told them to do. They got it done, too—somehow—and were out the gate and across to the ferry terminal just as they saw Joe and the Cessna lift off. As for the wirecutters, Mara had thrown them into enough dense vegetation and far enough away from the fence to make sure it would be years before they would be found.

"He tipped his wing. Yup. He tipped it," Sal said, her voice breaking. "Oh, how I love that man."

Chapter Sixteen

On the Move

With the onshore sleepovers and scheduling gaps Sal had designed to make tracking them more difficult, the trip to Kodiak would take four full days. Reasoning that it would be more secure, Sal had also made it clear that she and Mara were to act like they didn't know each other.

When they arrived at the ticket counter in Juneau, both paid full fare rather than use the lifetime pass Joe had given to Mara so as to avert any unnecessary attention. And, even though each stateroom had from two to four bunks in it, they each retired to separate quarters at different ends of the ferry.

Once en route, they made sure to meet and talk in an inconspicuous way—like leaning over the railing to watch something in the water, or brushing past each other in the cafeteria line. Mostly though, they avoided interacting altogether. They had also turned off their cell phones. There was no signal anyway, but even so, Sal was adamant that any potential for tracking them be eliminated.

For Mara, being on the ferry again had brought with it a rush of memories. It was on the ferry she had first seen Alaska, first met Doug and Thor, and it was on the ferry where Joe Michael had first given her the feather.

Since that first trip north from Bellingham, she had traveled often on the marine highway system, sometimes just for pleasure, but several times on the run from danger, just as she was now. She could think of other ways to travel, but none as unique and close to Alaska living as this was.

Cordova had been quiet during the stop there. With Sal napping, as she tended to do most afternoons anymore, Mara had ignored any risks and walked into town alone, taking pains to avoid the harbor area, where she was most likely to be recognized.

Her little sojourn had been less carefree than she would have liked because she had been unable to shake the image of both Doug and Sergeant Smith admonishing her for putting herself out there like this, but nothing had happened and the stroll around town had lifted her spirits.

Once back in her stateroom, she took the bag of taffy she had purchased from a small shop downtown out of her jacket pocket and quickly unwrapped and ate several pieces. She loved taffy, especially the ginger-flavored variety you could only get in Seward, but this was good, leaving her no reason to complain, except maybe about the spasm in her jaw that told her enough was enough of the sweet treat for now.

Their arrival in Whittier began the complicated leg of the trip because they needed to get to Homer on the road system, but Justin Smith had helped with that part by arranging for Stovepipe to send one of his men in a tow truck to pick them up and deliver them to the end of the road, where the ferry out of Homer would take them first to Kodiak, and then to Dutch Harbor. And so the rest of their journey began.

~ ~ ~

"Stovepipe says you're Doug William's old lady—er, sorry—I meant no disrespect," Smitty said, while leaning a bit to the right to shift gears.

"No offense Mr.—"

"Smitty. I don't answer to much else," he chuckled.

It was weird sitting in the big, lumbering tow truck, but Smitty was genial and easy to talk to, even though for much of the three-hour drive to Homer she was left with little to do but to stare out the window, while a blaring cd of Elvis's greatest hits drowned out any potential there might have been for conversation.

"That's why he was the King," Smitty suddenly said after singing along to *Are You Lonesome Tonight* on its third go-around on the CD player.

Mara watched Smitty rub his shirtsleeve across one eye, surprised to see someone as crusty as him tearing up.

"If you think I'm bad, you oughtta see ole Stovepipe when the King is on," Smitty volunteered after seeing the look of bewilderment on her face. "Sometimes work at the shop shuts right down if someone turns up the music. Sure enough does. That's why we usually keep the CDs all in the wreckers—just so we can get some work done."

Mara nodded, noting that Sal had dozed off once again in her place on the front seat between them. Apparently Elvis had lulled her into a comfortable place, too.

"This one really tears me up," Smitty said, as Elvis began singing *Danny Boy*. "I can almost feel my heart skipping at the sound of it."

Mara stared out the window at the dense foliage that lined the roadway, letting herself get lost in glimpses of the silty, turquoise Kenai River, while Elvis and Smitty sang *Danny Boy* inside the huge wrecker that was usually used to tow semis.

She closed her eyes, blocking out the near misses from which the narrow, shoulderless road offered little in the way of protection. Smitty took the curves unfazed as time and again they were sandwiched between oncoming traffic and the unforgiving guardrail that for some unknown reason had been installed directly over the white line on the right-hand side of the road.

Obviously Smitty was well versed in the intricacies of navigating the harrowing road that he told her had been slated for repair for so long all speculation about anyone ever fixing it had become a local joke. When she opened her eyes again, Elvis was done singing and the tow truck was heading down Baycrest Hill into Homer.

"This is where it's gonna get dicey," Smitty said. "There's a couple of semis coming in on the ferry we're gonna help to unload, so I'm gonna want you two ladies to just sit tight. Once we get down on the turn-stile, you're gonna need to hop out and head up the stairs, where the purser will take you to your rooms. That way, no one should even get a glimpse of you in Homer."

"Okay," Mara answered for both herself and for Sal.

"But don't we have to check in or something?" Sal asked, suddenly wide-awake.

"It's all taken care of," Smitty answered. "That's the word I got. It's all taken care of."

Sure enough, once in the stairwell up to the main deck, the two women were met by none other than Justin Smith, who briefed them on the latest developments (there were none) and handed them the necessary paperwork authorizing their travel—paperwork that Mara noted was signed by an individual from the Department of Homeland Security as well as a captain from the FBI.

Suddenly her knees felt like Jello and she could feel herself slumping against a wall, after which she slid down to the floor. When she woke up, she was lying on a stretcher in a room next to the purser's office.

"You're okay, now," the purser told her. "You just fainted. Your friend here said it happens whenever you get really nervous. You feeling all right now?"

Mara sat up, and then stood slowly.

"Yes, I guess it does," she answered. "Seems I've had to say that a lot lately."

Chapter Seventeen

What's Wrong?

"You're definitely not pregnant," the doctor who had been called on board by Justin Smith told Mara. "Which is probably a good thing, considering all that is going on here."

She didn't know him and he gave no sign of recognizing her, even though they both lived in Homer.

Whether it was from a sense of relief or a sense of disappointment, Mara burst into tears. She needed, Doug right now and he was off on the seiner with god knows who.

Sal was somewhat comforting, although her pragmatic take on things was a bit less fuzzy than Mara was hoping for right now.

"Hell's afire, Jane, all you need is a danged kid to worry about with everything else that's going on."

Of course, Sal was right, but did she have to be so blunt? Why was she feeling so sensitive about it anyway? She and Doug had long known that children were not in their future. Still, maybe a tiny part of her had always wondered if she would be a good mother and if Doug and she as a couple would be good parents. Those thoughts had always been fleeting, though, and even now she could feel reality check in. As had always been the case, she—and Doug along with her—were okay either way. That was something she loved about him, his ability to be in sync with her feelings.

"Do you have any explanation for the fainting, doctor?" she asked.

"Without further testing it's impossible to be certain," he answered. "But I'm willing to make a pretty good assumption that it's your blood sugar. The results just came back in and your blood glucose was about fifty percent of what it should be. Have you been eating in the mornings? I notice that both episodes happened in the morning or early afternoon."

"Just a donut and coffee," she answered.

"Try eating protein instead," he said. "This is acting like transient hypoglycemia. The protein will stick with you longer and hopefully prevent these sudden drops in glucose."

"But it doesn't happen every day . . ."

"Only when you put demands on your metabolism—like during times of intense stress or physical activity, right?"

"Yes," she answered after thinking about it. "That does seem to be the case."

"Try eating protein instead of sweets in the morning and if the symptoms return or continue, or worse yet, if they worsen, we'll do an in-depth workup. I think we found the culprit, though, with these test results. Matter of fact, I'm highly confident you will be just fine, but here's my card in case you want to follow up when you get back."

"I stuck my neck out and got you a BLT from the cafeteria, Jane," Sal said. "Now eat up, 'cause this is no time for medical drama, you hear?"

"Okay," Mara answered. "It looks delicious. Thanks."

Chapter Eighteen

Dutch

Once in Dutch Harbor, Mara stopped briefly at the hotel where she had once been treated like a castoff. Now, only a few years later, the proprietor all but begged her to stay there again, but Sal had other plans.

"I appreciate your generosity after what happened and all, but I know someone who knows someone," she announced on behalf of the two of them.

So much for pretending they didn't know each other.

When Mara met up with Doug and Derrk, it was under cover of night, and only in passing along the well-traveled waterfront. She and Sal had already agreed to meet up later after Sal had had time to make arrangements for them to stay in some cabins located near the edge of town.

"I hate living this way," Doug said as he finally let Mara's hand slip away from his. "I didn't dare let Thor off the seiner for fear he'd never leave you to come back to me."

As she walked by, Mara heard Thor whimper the almost imperceptible sound he used to communicate only with her. She answered back, letting the sound, "Uh uh," come from deep within her heart. Thor understood that sound and knew to be quiet and let her walk away without trying to get out to her as she and Doug both knew he would try to do.

"I actually crated him," he told her. "It was hard to do."

"He knows I'll be back," she answered.

Their next visit was better, with the couple spending two whole days in the cabin Sal had found, while Sal went off reconnecting with old friends from the local fishing community, where she was well known as Sal Kindle.

The person who returned was the same gritty old woman who had long sprinkled Mara's consciousness with her salty rhetoric and who had actually turned out to be the well-heeled Sylvia LaMonte of Rhinebeck, New York, while the man who left had been reminded that he was married to the one woman he would do anything for in life, and who he knew felt the same way about him.

Doug and Derrk would be off to the Bering Sea in the morning and the next time Mara would see her husband would be right back here in Dutch Harbor in about three weeks—god willing.

When Mara heard the scratch on her door the next morning, she knew it was Thor, just as she knew Doug had had a change of heart and set him loose before leaving. In true Thor fashion, the wolf dog put his front paws up onto her shoulders and pushed his nose against hers to kiss her, before sitting politely on the floor.

"Could be my friend's gonna hassle us a bit about ole Thor," Sal muttered before declaring, "Well, danged if he does anyway. He's yer dog and that's that, so I'll take care of any problems if they crop up."

Mara smiled at the way Sal had reverted to her crusty persona. Her smile broadened when Sal scraped a pan full of fried beef strips onto a plate she had set on the floor for Thor.

"Not too much," Mara cautioned. "He knows he needs to eat his dog food, too."

The three of them stayed fairly closed in for the rest of the week, except for a visit from the owner of the cabins—an old man with leathery skin and piercing blue eyes, who Sal said could be trusted and who ultimately said he didn't mind Thor being there. Except for that visit, though, not much happened to disturb them.

Chapter Nineteen

Anna?

"Thor! Come!" Mara called sharply, but the wolf dog bounded away from her, running down the nearly empty street of an early Sunday morning along the waterfront of Dutch Harbor.

"Thor! Doggone it, Thor! C'mere! Come!"

Thor stopped momentarily to look back at Mara before darting between two buildings and then re-emerging alongside a dumpster, where he decided to relieve himself.

"Thor! Stop! You wanna get us fined?"

The dog was undeterred and ran back down a narrow alley, coming back out to summon Mara at least three times before she caught up with him, and was able to snap on his leash.

"I can't believe you!" she scolded him. "If this is how you're going to behave, then—"

She stopped short when she saw the silhouette of a young woman in the shadows. The girl must have been about eighteen, and by the looks of her tired gait, she had been traveling for several days.

"Quiet!" Mara whispered to Thor, who seemed determined to get to the young woman.

Before she could stop him, though, Thor broke loose from his leash and ran to the young woman, running in circles around her and then jumping up to lick her face.

"Thor!" Mara yelled. "Down!"

Suddenly the scene before her went into slow motion as the young woman slipped the huge backpack off her shoulders, bent down, and embraced Thor as if she would never let him go. When she looked up, Mara couldn't believe what she was seeing.

Anna looked back at her briefly before grabbing her backpack and running away from her.

"Stay, Thor!" she heard the familiar voice say. "Stay."

She had just talked to Ellie a couple of weeks ago when everything had seemed fine. Her and Ben's marriage was happy and secure and both had been very excited to know Anna was now finishing college up in Fairbanks.

"She's studying biology, just like you did," Ellie had said. "We haven't heard much from her except she loves her roommate and is carrying a heavy course schedule. She told us not to worry and she would be back home for Thanksgiving."

Mara sat on a bench that had been shoved out behind one of the shops that backed up to the alley. Anna had grown up so fast. Why, it seemed like only yesterday when she had been welcoming Ben as her new father and sharing her excitement about her mother's new-found happiness.

So much had happened in those years—too much for one lifetime. Now, here Mara was caught up in a new drama. Her plate was full by anyone's standards, and now, well, what was Anna doing in Dutch Harbor and why was she avoiding her?

She desperately wanted to call Ellie to find out if she and Ben knew Anna was in Dutch. But, maybe it was legit, you know. Maybe it was a field trip for college, or a sabbatical, or whatever.

Besides, risking a call to Ellie would blow her own cover and that was a chance she could not take right now.

"C'mon, Thor," she called to her dog, surprised when he followed her without trying to go after Anna.

Chapter Twenty

Huh?

Mara tossed and turned all night. Why would Anna be in Dutch Harbor and apparently alone, and why would she not acknowledge someone who was as close to her as she was? Sure, there was the whole potential that this was about college and sabbaticals and so forth, but Anna was still in grad school and could not possibly be ready for such an assignment. Besides, they were close. They had always been close. The Anna she knew would never behave this way.

Maybe Anna was in Dutch earning money for college, but Mara knew with certainty that Ben and Ellie had provided funding for her studies long ago. And it was October, too early for her to have flunked out of school if that was the case—not that this could even be a remote possibility.

She told Doug about it when he called later, using the satellite phone he always carried at sea.

"This'll be it for a couple of weeks," he warned her. "We're heading into thirty-foot seas and they're saying it could get worse, depending on what happens with the typhoon coming out of Japan."

Mara listened as Doug went on, telling her about their plan to shelter in a small cove he favored near Nushagak if it looked like the weather was going to fail.

"Stopping there will set us back about two days," he told her, "but safety first and always."

The news about the weather made Mara cringe and she wanted to call Doug home—think of an emergency or something to get him back her way. She quickly discarded the plan. Doug would never tolerate her pulling something like that.

She reminded herself of how they had decided to live their dreams, even after inheriting more money last year than they would ever use. She needed to trust Doug. He was as experienced as anyone out there, and he was known to surround himself with equally experienced help. He was also well regarded in the fishing community, and though he seldom asked for help, if ever he did, there would be more than he needed coming his way.

And then there was the situation with Joey and those who apparently were out to do the young man harm. Wasn't it just like Doug to help his friend, Derrk, and to help the police, even despite the attempt that had been made on his own life?

"I'll always worry when you're away," she said, trying to have the last word on his travels. "So what do you make of the Anna thing?"

"I don't know. She's an adult now, but . . ."

"I know."

"But still, why would she try to run from you? I guess that's the big mystery here."

"That's right," Mara agreed.

"You're gonna have to try to find her," Doug said. "But, and this is a big but, Mara, you need to promise me you'll watch your back."

"I will," she answered.

"I mean it, Mara. It's obvious we're not dealing with entry-level thugs here. You be careful—and just for GP, tell Justin Smith about Anna."

"You couldn't possibly think she's involved in this somehow, could you?" Mara said, feeling a bit of panic.

"Not at all," Doug answered, "although you and I both know just about anything's possible in this life we live. I just think he should be aware she exists and she's in Dutch, that's all. Gut feeling."

The two talked for a bit longer before hanging up, leaving Mara in need of a walk.

"C'mere, Thor," she called, watching the moosehide medallion with the wolf head stitched in quills and blue iridescent beads dangle from his collar.

In all the years that Thor had worn it, it had only gotten better with age. Della's mother, Mary, had done a good job on it. Joe Michael's first wife, Betty, had been Mary's twin. Meeting Mary was probably kind of like meeting Betty.

Joe had never really gotten over losing Betty in the fire, so Mara had learned not to bring her name up to him. Besides, he had finally found a semblance of happiness with Sal. Deep inside, though, she had always wanted to learn more about the woman Joe Michael had been married to for longer than she had even been alive, and so meeting Mary had helped her to piece together a vision of what Betty must have been like.

If Betty was anything like Mary, then she had been a good woman. Mara fingered the quill bracelet Mary had given her in appreciation for helping save Della's life after gang leader Carlos Antoya had robbed the motel where Della had been working, and after which he had shot her and left her on the ground to die—bleeding.

That bracelet was something she treasured almost as much as she did the feather with the red dot painted on it, given to her by Joe Michael, and which was currently missing somewhere in Hoonah. For that reason alone, she double-checked the clasp on the wristlet and pulled a sleeve down over it to protect it, all the while wondering if seeing Anna was what had put her into such a sentimental mood.

Chapter Twenty-One

Across a Cup of Macchiato

Mara found Anna sooner than she had expected to. "Are you avoiding me for some reason, Anna?" she said as she slid into a chair beside her at the coffee shop down by the harbor.

She watched a deep flush wash over the young woman's face and took a sip of macchiato before placing the tiny porcelain cup back into its saucer.

"I see," Mara said softly when Anna didn't answer. "How about if we talk about it, okay?"

Anna looked up and nodded meekly, while Mara reached over and patted her hand.

"You've grown up, Anna. I can't believe you're a young woman now. It seems like just yesterday —well, you know."

"Please don't tell my mom or Ben," Anna pleaded. "They think I'm still in grad school up in Fairbanks."

"Okay," Mara answered, not asking the one burning question she had about why Anna was not in school. "But you know they love you and they would be worried sick if they knew."

"I know," Anna replied, reaching down to stroke Thor's head.

"So, what *is* going on, Anna?"

"I met someone, Aunt Mara. A guy. Now before you judge me, just listen," Anna said, her voice taking on a stressed and slightly embarrassed-sounding tone.

"Okay. Well, you're twenty-one now, Anna. Things like that can happen. I mean, I ran off with Brad for a few months when I was your age. But then my parents found out—it was a different time then, you know."

Anna didn't answer. Instead, she jumped up to go get herself a bottled water from the cooler.

Mara sipped her macchiato, watching the young woman, who seemed to have been caught doing something even she wasn't sure she wanted to be involved in.

"Anna! Let's go," a male voice called from the open door.

Mara looked up to see a young man as handsome as he was tall calling to Anna. Anna set her drink down and moved toward him, while Mara reached down to calm Thor, who had let out a low growl at the sight of the young man.

"I gotta go," Anna said, looking back nervously. "Don't worry. I'm fine."

"Wait. Anna. Your coat," Mara called, reaching around to take the young woman's coat off the back of a chair.

"I got it. Thanks," The young man said, walking over to take it from Mara. "C'mon, Anna."

Mara sat back down, but not before stooping to pick up a piece of paper that had fallen out of Anna's pocket. By now, both Anna and the young man were out of sight. She stared at the paper for what seemed like a full five minutes before making her decision to look at it. After all, what if it was something important?

She picked up another macchiato at the counter and sat back down with Thor at her feet. She loved that the owners allowed dogs inside— at least no one had asked her to take him back out.

She sipped her coffee and slowly unfolded the white paper with light blue lines that had obviously been torn from a spiral book of some kind.

The paper consisted of a list of names and phone numbers, including those for Anna's parents, her dorm and presumably her school, along with several other names she didn't recognize—that is, until she saw the last two, listed under the names *Joey* and *Q.T.*

A shiver ran up her spine. Why couldn't she stop trembling? She dialed Doug's satellite phone, but was unable to make a connection.

"What's wrong, Jane?" Sal said as she joined her in the coffee shop. "You look like ya seen the proverbial ghost."

Chapter Twenty-Two

Oppression

"Here's your pancakes, Uncle Joe," Della said, handing her uncle a heaping plate of his favorite breakfast food.

"I appreciate your efforts, niece," Joe Michael told her. "And the fact you actually listened to me and came here to Juneau."

"Well, I mean, you said it's not safe in Hoonah. Anyway, I'm thinking of going up to see my mother in Glenallen. She's been sick, you know. Cancer."

"I didn't know, Della."

"Henry's been taking good care of her."

"He's a good man," Joe answered.

"I think I need to be there."

"Okay. Do you need any money? Does your mother or Henry?"

"No. We're okay. Thanks," Della answered.

"Well, just let me know if you do, honey."

"I will, Uncle Joe."

"I think I'm going to head back to Hoonah next week," Joe said. "Sal's in Dutch Harbor with Mara—well, you already knew that—and I got things to do at home. Yup. Plenty of things to do, the main one being finding that danged feather."

"I don't think you should go there," Della said.

"Now don't go getting all motherly on me, Della. And whatever you do, don't tell your Aunt Sal—or Mara."

"I won't, Uncle Joe, but I think you should stay here."

"You don't understand, Della. I need that feather."

"You're going to find it," Della said matter-of-factly. "When it's time."

Joe Michael got up and carried his empty dish to the sink. His life was virtually ruled by all the women in it and it angered him that he loved them all too much to disrespect them and do what he really wanted to do.

"Don't be mad, Uncle Joe," Della said.

"I'm not mad, Della," he answered. "The last thing I want to do is to cause you, Mara, or god forbid, my loving wife, Sal, a moment's worry. Danged women anyway, just can't let a man be a man what with all the mothering. Anyway, I won't go to Hoonah for now, Della. I promise."

"Thanks, Uncle Joe," Della answered. "I'm gonna go pack now. And I think I'll make up some lunches for you for the freezer."

"Okay, Della. Thanks."

"No worries, Uncle Joe. Aunt Sal told me you don't like to cook."

Chapter Twenty-Three

Their Plan

Larry Allen Kenton threw several wrenches and a couple of pry bars onto the table next to the long, cluttered workbench that served as his office, clearing a workspace before reaching behind the collection of diesel manuals onto a secret shelf that held his black, leather-bound book of notes.

For whatever it was worth, he ran a rag across the area in front of him and over the stool in front of it before sitting down—careful not to wrinkle his freshly ironed khakis or the sleeves of his crisply starched dress shirt as he flipped through the pages that contained handwritten entries from the myriad cases he had investigated over the years.

"I've seen that logo before," he told the tall, neatly dressed blond woman, who stood behind him twisting her hair up into a chignon. "Seriously, Jocelyn, I know the information about the scarves is somewhere in this volume or the other one I keep in the house. I'm sure of it, I just need to find it."

"They're sending me down to Dutch Harbor," Capt. Jocelyn Sanders answered. "Tell Ted and all the guys old Stormy's gone south to visit her mother, okay?"

Jocelyn Sanders's mouth tweaked slightly and a momentary twinkle flickered in her eyes as Sgt. Larry Kenton laughed at her wry comment. Leaning over, he rubbed his calf where the stovepipe he had been wearing as a disguise had caused a large blister to pop just this morning.

"Just in case you need me, I'll be down in California visiting my daughter for a couple of weeks. I'll have my private phone, and of course, my business phone for old Stovepipe. Meanwhile, Ted'll be in charge here and he'll know how to find me just in case Stovepipe's girlfriend, Chloe Pearl Jean "Stormy" Maxwell comes looking for him."

This time, Larry Kenton's laugh was full and hearty as he watched Jocelyn Sanders's mouth curl slowly into a half smile and her eyes twinkle in amusement at the obvious reference to their undercover personas.

In truth, although she and Larry Kenton could probably qualify for an academy award for their carefully crafted disguises, outside of work, they made an almost extreme effort to avoid each other. Had her smile meant that perhaps there had been a slight thawing in her affection for the man she had once sworn to see in hell after—well, he knew why.

"Are you sure Ted doesn't have a clue about my real identity?" Jocelyn asked.

"I'm positive," Larry Kenton answered. "There is some information in this line of work even a person's lifelong partner and best friend is better off not knowing about—just so the system can work, you know."

"I'll be meeting up with a special agent from Homer named Sgt. Justin Smith," Jocelyn continued. "He's been coordinating the investigation since the murder happened down there. I'm guessing the cops down there are going to be pretty surprised to learn this is now a federal matter."

"Undoubtedly," Larry Kenton replied before standing to show Jocelyn to the door, where a gray Mercedes coupe had been left for her last night.

"I'll be in touch," she said crisply, withdrawing her hand from his own once he had helped her into the car.

"Safe travels, Captain Sanders," Sergeant Kenton said as she pulled away.

"And god help poor Sgt. Justin Smith for getting stuck with her steely self as a supervisor," he said to Ted.

Chapter Twenty-Four

More Than A Limerick?

Since he wasn't going to Hoonah, Joe Michael decided to go to Sitka to see how things were going with the totem-raising plans. Instead of flying, though, he took the ferry, carrying an insulated bag of snacks Della had prepared for him.

The day was beautiful and unseasonably warm. There was little wind, which made it a pleasure to sit outside on one of the benches that lined the decks. As the ferry turned south into Chatham Strait and made its way alongside the eastern edge of Chichagof Island, then across Peril Strait and down the western edge of Baranof Island toward Sitka, he basked in the sun and the sea breeze that was his life's blood.

Despite the years he had ridden the Alaska Marine Highway, Joe Michael had never grown tired of either the ferry or the unparalleled views of Southeast Alaska.

For a while, a pod of Dall porpoises had swum alongside the ferry, frolicking and cavorting in the vessel's wake as if they hadn't a care in the world. Joe had even seen a couple of humpbacks today, which was always a treat.

He took several deep breaths of the clean, fresh air as they moved along the millions of acres that made up the Tongass National Forest.

Everywhere he looked, the white heads of eagles dotted the trees. Once he thought he saw a black bear on the shore, but he hadn't brought binoculars, so he couldn't be totally sure—but he was pretty sure, and so he decided he had seen one.

Della had made him a huge lunch, which he thoroughly enjoyed from a bench on the outer deck as the ferry moved along. She was a wonderful cook, just like her mother. Betty had been their equal in the kitchen as well. It had been a long time since he had thought of his wife and the fire that took her life and the lives of their children. This time, though, he chose not to feel sad. Instead, he thought of how much he loved her and how well she had taken care of him and their family. Somewhere during his recollections, he fell asleep. Did he dream she visited him?

When he awoke, all thoughts of Betty were gone—vanquished to the years-ago memory of his former life. He was Sal's husband now and he loved her unconditionally. He closed his eyes and willed her to be safe; throwing in an extra wish Mara would be safe, too.

As he folded up the bag that once held his lunch, a small paper fell to the deck. He snatched it up before it could blow away. On one side was a drawing of the aurora, and on the other, four lines written in a hand that was both steady and meticulous.

Dilly Dally Sally
Ho Ho Joe
Hope you still love me
Once you get to know.

Whatever in the world was this? It wasn't like Della to be disrespectful, but this was obviously her handwriting. Was she trying to tease him? Play some kind of game to amuse him?

He stuffed the paper into his breast pocket. Della certainly had a dry sense of humor, but this was not the greatest example of it for sure. He imagined she had been trying to cheer him up, maybe even practicing limericks on him. She had often told him how much she admired his ability to write limericks.

Della had recently told him she had been restless of late upon on learning her legal troubles were apt to go on for several more years, and also upon hearing that her mother had been diagnosed with cancer.

She had probably been messing around and accidentally put the paper in his lunch bag. He folded it up and placed it in his pocket. He'd make sure she got it back when they met up again, and hopefully, the two of them would share a good laugh about her attempt at writing. *Hopefully* was the key word and hopefully this was a joke.

Chapter Twenty-Five

The Test

When he walked into the atrium at Totem Park looking for his friend, John, Joe Michael could see John's son putting the finishing touches on the red cedar totem pole that lay lengthwise on a covered deck outside. It was supported by a series of logs that had grooves cut out to support the weight of the 60-foot-tall memorial pole John and his son had designed to tell the story of John's generation.

John had chosen Joe Michael to carve his own special story within the saga of the pole, so Joe had carved a curved feather against a back drop of the sun and with a red dot about a third of the way down on the outer side. He had chosen a special mixture of local berries, salmon roe, and other binding agents to create the exact color of red he desired—one that reflected the depth and intensity of all emotion, and for which he had purposely used the ancient coloring technique of his people.

From his vantage point, he couldn't see the red dot, so he walked outside, nodding to John's son and walking around the totem to look at his work. He was astonished to see the red dot was gone and the edges of the feather had been smoothed over to look like extended rays of the image of the sun he had carved beneath the feather.

Wide-eyed, he looked up at John's son, who continued to work without acknowledging him. He leaned over and touched the pole and felt the roughness where his carving had been altered. Then he picked up a chisel, and other carving tools and began to return the totem to its original form—all this while John's son continued working without speaking. Then, late in the day and as the sun was setting he stood, nodded at John's son, and walked away.

"It was a test to see if you would return," John said from behind where Joe Michael stood.

"It was a necessary thing," John continued. "Part of the story."

Joe Michael turned to his friend and nodded, understanding even within the parameters of the anger he felt at having seen his work destroyed.

"Somehow I will have to find the berries and the roe to recreate the color in time for the ceremony," Joe Michael said, before remembering he had stashed a small glass jar with some remaining paint inside a hollowed log just in case he should need it again.

Walking into the woods a bit, he retrieved the jar and brought it back.

"It's like you knew," John said.

Joe Michael stared at John, amazed at the wisdom shown by his oldest friend. He wished he could be so wise—so centered and focused and directed. But he had struggled through much of his life, often overcome by the challenges of dealing with the tragedies that had befallen him, and had rendered him unable to see with the clarity possessed by his friend John.

He used his fingers to smudge the red dye over the dot, spitting some of his own saliva onto them to make the color flow. When he was done, he wiped his hands with the handkerchief he carried in his back pocket, and then stuffed it back into his pants in case he needed it again.

"I see trouble on your face, my friend," John said softly. "And I also see determination to overcome it. The pole-raising ceremony will wait until you are ready and the fact you will be ready is as certain to me as are those stars are beginning to emerge in this night's sky."

Joe Michael walked up to his friend and placed one hand on his shoulder, before walking down the path that led out of Totem Park, while John stood watching—as if a guardian of his friend's legacy.

Chapter Twenty-Six

Police "Present"

"Justin? I hadn't realized that you were the Sergeant Smith attached to this case. So nice to see you again."

"And you as well, Jocelyn," Justin Smith answered. "So what brings you to Dutch Harbor?"

Jocelyn Smith brushed the wrinkles from her linen skirt before removing a cigarette from a jeweled case and extending it from her lip for Justin Smith to light.

"Sorry, Mom, but I can't support you on this," he answered.

"Just can it with the 'mom' thing, would you, Justin? Step mothers don't count."

"Okay, Jocelyn, but if Dad were alive and knew I was helping you support this filthy habit, then I don't think either of us would be standing here right now."

"Well, your father, god rest his soul, was well aware I smoked, just as he was well aware that the fact he died in prison was a pretty significant contributor to my need to do so just to keep my sanity."

Justin Smith reached for a lighter, lit Jocelyn's cigarette, put the lighter away, and then stared at the ground. It was true what she said. His father had died in prison after living his life as a low-level drug runner and a repeat offender.

Justin had been only six years old when his mother had—as his father told him— "gone to heaven, so cry your tears, boy, and let's get on with our lives."

Two years later he had married Jocelyn Sanders, whom he had met at a strip club in East St. Louis. To her credit, she had stopped working in order to stay home and care for the young boy, and Justin had grown up not only calling her Mom, but discovering she was the only stable force in his life.

He couldn't remember exactly when it was that Jocelyn had gotten her high school diploma and then, first her bachelor's, and then master's in criminal justice. He knew it was while he was in high school, because they had graduated together—a poignant moment for them both.

He had gone on to become a street cop before pursuing his degree in criminal justice and joining the FBI, but Jocelyn had gone full-steam ahead in forging her own exemplary career.

Somewhere along life's path, the two had parted ways, losing all contact with each other over some silly tiff, and with neither of them seeming to mind. Only recently had he learned she was a special agent for the FBI, and she he was an FBI agent himself.

They had met for lunch last Christmas and promised to stay in touch. Like the flight of warm ambiance that marks so many Christmases, they hadn't spoken to or seen each other since.

"I guess I should tell you formally that I am—well, formally—the lead investigator on this case," Jocelyn Sanders said. "Although you will retain the title of Incident Commander, you will report to me and coordinate all your efforts with me. Just so you're clear, you know?"

"Would you like me to refer to you as Captain or as Mom?" Justin sniped.

Not missing a beat, Jocelyn replied, "We've already established that I'm not your mother, and our age difference is too great for me to accept your using my first name, so I guess *captain* it will be."

Jocelyn stuffed her cigarette butt into a nearby container before turning back to face Justin Smith.

"I'll need to be briefed on the current status of your investigation, including contact information for all the players in this little adventure, sergeant. Once that is completed, perhaps you'd like to accompany me to that fancy hotel across town for dinner—just for old time's sake, you know?"

"I'll have a full report for you in the morning, Captain Sanders, but as for dinner, well, I'm going to be tied up doing—I don't know—something else this evening, but thank you so kindly for the invitation."

"Sure, Justin. I understand," Jocelyn Sanders replied.

Chapter Twenty-Seven

Anna!

"That's an interesting development with your young friend, Anna," Justin Smith told Mara over coffee. "It seems to me that we might want to look into the identity of this young man she seems to be traveling with."

After going on to explain the increased scope of the investigation and the presence of Capt. Jocelyn Sanders, he offered her his new card, which held the additional contact information.

"Anything, anything at all that seems out of the ordinary, please text me," he told her. "Even if it seems insignificant. Meanwhile, hopefully you'll meet up with your young friend soon and I've got a feeling that that would be a good thing all the way around."

It was less than three hours later when Mara ran into Anna in the local grocery store. This time, Anna was alone and seemed to be wandering the aisles in a meandering way that caught Mara's attention. After watching her for a bit, she approached her.

"Anna?"

Anna jumped.

"I didn't mean to startle you, Anna."

"I was just daydreaming, Aunt Mara."

"Where's your friend?" Mara asked.

"We broke up," Anna answered.

Mara put one arm around the young woman.

"I'm sorry. I know how much that hurts."

"It's okay," Anna answered. "Things weren't going that well anyway."

"Are you hungry," Mara asked. "I was thinking of going to the hotel for dinner."

"I can't really—I don't have enough—"

"My treat," Mara said.

She watched as Anna retrieved her large backpack from the entry to the store before joining her on the walk along the harbor.

"Is this all your stuff?" Mara asked.

"Just about," Anna answered, hesitating, and then adding, "He broke the rest."

"Like what?" Mara asked, trying to keep from sounding angry.

"Just my phone and my iPad," Anna said.

"Do you have a place to stay?"

"No. I was going to sleep inside the lobby here," Anna answered. "Then see if they would let me call my mom."

Both women stopped talking long enough to order, which came as a welcome relief to Mara because it gave her a moment to think.

Once the waiter had delivered her glass of wine, she took several sips before asking the question she was most afraid to ask.

"Did he do anything to hurt you?" she said.

Tears welled in Anna's eyes as she looked away. Those tears were quickly followed by more tears, which soon broke into wrenching sobs.

"He told me he loved me, Aunt Mara. He promised we'd be together forever. He said nothing else mattered, college didn't matter, and no one would ever love me like he did."

Mara handed the young woman a tissue and let her cry.

"At first everything was okay. We were so in love. Every day was special. But then, he started getting upset—first about little things, and then about just about everything. I begged him to tell me what I was doing wrong, but he would just throw something and stomp out the door. He always came back, though, even if it was a couple of days later. And he always said he was sorry. Things would be okay for a while and then it would happen again. When he broke my phone, I decided to leave. That's when you found me in the store."

"What are your plans for now?" Mara asked.

"I don't know. I guess I need to call my mom and find a way to get home." Anna grabbed Mara's hand.

"She's going to be so angry, Aunt Mara. And Ben. Ben will probably come down here and—"

"Okay. Settle down, Anna. It's getting late. Do you think he'll come looking for you—this guy?"

"I don't think so. He was going out for a week with one of the seiners starting this afternoon. His buddies are all deckhands and one of them got him a job on a boat called the *Driftfeather*. OMG, Aunt Mara! Isn't that one of Uncle Doug's boats?"

Mara's mind was racing. Doug and Derrk were supposed to have gone out yesterday. Something must have happened to keep them in Nushagak an extra day.

"They were supposed to have gone out yesterday," she told Anna.

"I know, but they had to wait to hire more crew. That's how Cory got the job," Anna said. "He said they were flying him to Nushagak last time I saw him."

Chapter Twenty-Eight

OMG, No!

Even knowing there was no way to warn Doug, Mara tried anyway, dialing the satellite phone over and over to no avail. She closed her eyes and willed him to know her thoughts. He would get them. She just knew he would.

Again, habitually as always, she reached for the feather before her conscious mind reminded her that it was lost. She closed her eyes again, willing even harder for her thoughts to go to Doug. Did he hear her frantic message to be careful? Could he feel her warning like she had so often felt his?

She texted Justin Smith.

PLEASE MEET ME ASAP IN THE COFFEE SHOP NEXT TO THE HARBOR.

To her surprise, he was waiting for her when she arrived.

"Wow, you really meant it when you said you'd be there for me if I texted, didn't you?"

"This is serious business, Mrs. Williams. What's going on?"

Mara ordered her drink and proceeded to tell Justin Smith what Anna had told her.

"And now I learn that this Cory guy might be on Doug's seiner, the *Driftfeather*. I'm scared, sergeant. Really scared."

"I'll get word to him," Justin Smith answered.

"But how . . .?" Mara let her words trail off.

"Isn't the *Driftfeather* about due for an unannounced Coast guard inspection?" Justin Smith said, winking as he stood up.

"But—" Mara began.

"And I've got other plans in place. Things I can't tell you about right now. Please trust me, Mrs. Williams. If this kid Cory makes a wrong move, he'll be returning to the mainland sooner than he planned."

Mara sighed, took a deep breath and sighed again.

"Try to stay calm, Mrs. Williams—Mara—try to trust me on this."

"I'm trying to, but it's hard," Mara answered.

"We need to let this play out. See what comes down. I'm not sure just yet what all this involves, but my gut tells me it's bigger than Doug and either the *Storm Roamer* or the *Driftfeather*—bigger than Derrk, Joey, or your young friend, Anna. Excuse me . . ."

Justin Smith reached into his pocket and pulled out his phone.

"Yes, captain. Right away," he said before hanging up.

"I've gotta go," he told Mara.

Mara watched the only person she could trust with her husband's fate walk out into the street. Then, to her horror, she saw him spin around, then fall limply to the ground.

Her screams were matched by the screams of every other person in the room, some of whom rushed into the street in a fervent attempt to help the young officer.

"He's been shot!" someone hollered.

"It's too late," an ashen-faced stranger told those inside as the shop manager locked the door behind him.

Moments later an ambulance arrived, followed immediately by more police cars than it seemed a small town like this would possess. Mara watched them work in slow motion, waiting along with everyone else inside the small shop until officials could take everyone's witness statements.

Chapter Twenty-Nine

Pure and Simple Fear

Mara stayed off to the side, unable to ignore the snippets of conversation in the small coffee shop that had now become a crime scene.

"He's one of the suits that come around following trouble, that's all I know. A narc or something . . ."

"I've seen him in here before . . ."

"He was sitting with . . ." (hushed tones)

Mara heard the whispers and turned uncomfortably as several people looked her way.

"She's been hanging around here lately . . ."

"Always some woman leading a man to an early demise," said a bearded man with long hair that hadn't been combed in a while.

"Like you're a sainted angel yourself, Roland?" another grizzled-looking guy replied.

"I told ya to call me Otter if I told ya once already, ya slimy piece of muktuk-chewin' dumb post," Otter said, pushing his chair back and getting up from the table.

"Sit it down, Otter, and keep it planted before I tie ya to that chair," another of the small group of men at his table told him.

The barista—a young woman with thick hair hanging in a long braid down her back—brought a cup of coffee to Mara and sat down beside her.

"Just ignore them," she said. "We all do. They're a good bunch, really, but sometimes I think they need to get off the island and into civilization a bit more often."

"Thank you," Mara answered. "You know, for the coffee, and the company."

She glanced at the window. A couple of photographers wearing police vests, were taking photos of Justin Smith, who lay sprawled face down on the sidewalk outside the shop. Off to the side, a couple of officers were talking with a stout-looking woman, who Mara had seen show a badge to the group.

The woman approached Justin Smith, nodded, removed his cell phone from his now limp hand, placed it into an envelope, and handed a piece of paper to one of the officers.

Who was she? Everyone seemed to be deferring to her.

Mara turned away so as not to stare, but found herself looking back just in time to see the woman lean over and gently stroke Justin Smith's hair before standing and walking to a waiting black suburban.

"The cops take it hard when they lose one of their own," the barista said.

Mara didn't answer; instead, she sipped her coffee and said a prayer for Justin Smith. He had been such a nice guy. Dedicated, confident—obviously ethical and good. Who had gunned him down in broad daylight and why? Had it been a set-up? It had happened right after the phone call. And why had the woman taken his phone?

She looked away as they loaded Justin's body onto a gurney and took him away in an ambulance that sped away from the scene. Why the hurry? Wasn't he already on the fast train to eternity?

Her heart flip-flopped a couple of times in her chest. She drew in a deep breath as if to calm it, and then another before nodding to a police detective who had just sat down to take her statement.

No, she had never seen him before. Yes, he had sat at her table, but she thought he was just being friendly. Yes, he had mentioned his name. Her recollection was that it had been Jason or something—she wasn't sure. No, she didn't have her ID on her, did she need it because it was in her hotel room?

"I'm married, so I wasn't interested in any intense conversation," she told the investigator.

When the detective was done taking her statement, she left for the decoy hotel room that contained the fake ID Justin Smith had provided for her "in case the situation gets weird." He had known this was possible, hadn't he? She gave the detective the driver's license that bore her fake name. After taking down the information and telling her not to leave the area, he left.

How long would it take them to figure out her name wasn't really Alisa Allison and everything she had told them had been a lie born of the deep fear and mistrust that had overcome her?

She wandered around town till dark before going back to the cabin where Sal was beside herself waiting.

"Hell's afire, Jane. I mean, what the heck, anyway?"

Chapter Thirty

Past Present

"They killed him, Sal."

"What are you talking about, Mara? Killed who?"

"Justin Smith. Someone shot him dead in the street."

A knock at the door forestalled Sal's response.

"Well if it ain't my old friend, Stormy Maxwell," Sal exclaimed.

"Sal Kindle? You've gotta be kidding me!"

"That's right, Miss Stormy. Hey, where's my manners. Come in outta the cold already."

Jocelyn Sanders stepped inside the small cabin, immediately fixing her gaze on Mara.

"So, ya don't look like yer strippin' fer a livin' anymore, Stormy," Sal said, closing the door.

Jocelyn Sanders straightened her skirt.

"Those days are long gone, Sal. Although it's good to see an old friend, I'm here on official business now."

She handed Sal her card that read: CAPTAIN JOCELYN SANDERS, FEDERAL BUREAU OF INVESTIGATION SPECIAL AGENT.

"Ya gotta be kiddin' me, Stormy! Yer a cop? Hell's afire, anyway. Frozen hell's afire!"

"Been one for a while now, Sal. I was working undercover even back when you knew me."

"Wow!" Sal answered. "I never knew. You're good!"

"I've never forgotten you, Sal, and that day when you pushed me out of the way of the drunk with a knife, who thought I was evil incarnate for stripping."

"Anyone woulda done it, Stormy, but I knew you was a straight-up person back then and why, even though I've got a million questions about the fact you're one of the feds, that I'm invitin' ya to sit down to a cup of tea or whatever, okay?"

"I'm actually here to talk to Mrs. Williams," Captain Sanders said, looking over at the woman who was shifting uncomfortably and staring at the floor. "But a nice hot cup of tea does sound good, old friend."

Sal guided Jocelyn Sanders to a chair near the window and put the water on to boil.

"Mind if I smoke?" Captain Sanders asked. "It's an old habit I can't seem to break."

"Sure. Whatever," Sal answered, pushing an empty soda can across the table. "Guess this'll have to do for yer ashtray."

"On second thought, I'll just wait, Sal."

"Mrs. Williams?" Jocelyn Sanders asked, raising one eyebrow as she spoke. "Please join us."

Mara sat at the table with the two women, recognizing Captain Sanders as the woman she had seen lean over Justin Smith and stroke his hair.

Suddenly, Thor burst into the room, placing himself squarely in front of Mara, and then sitting at her feet.

"Nice dog," Captain Sanders said coolly.

"What the blazes is goin' on here, you two?" Sal said.

"I think your Mrs. Williams can explain this to you," Captain Sanders answered. "Why don't you tell Sal why you're using an alias and then maybe tell me why you're here with my old friend, Sal."

"How about if we all sit down and straighten some of this out?" Sal said. "Starting with me comin' forward with some truths of my own now that the law's involved."

By the time they had sipped the rest of their tea and enjoyed the coffee cake that Sal had made that morning, Sal had filled Jocelyn in on the fact that her real name was Sylvia LaMonte and that Mara was her daughter.

"But I wasn't working undercover like you were, Stormy. I was just hiding out from my family mostly—and for good reason, I might add."

Mara had listened to all of this without saying anything. When she finally did speak, both older women listened to her every word.

"Sergeant Smith was a good man. I trusted him. He was helping me. When I saw him gunned down in the street, I couldn't believe it. Who would do such a thing? Was it the same person who had roughed up Doug? The same person who was trying to incriminate Derrk's son, Joey? Was it the person who had murdered the person whose dead body had become entangled in ropes and seaweed back in Homer?"

She paused for several minutes as if to think.

"Justin Smith had warned me that weird things could start happening. That's why he had set me up with an alias and a hotel room—just in case. I panicked when I saw him gunned down. I was terrified. He had just taken a call from someone and then it happened. Was that person waiting outside? Waiting for me? Were the police part of it? I couldn't be sure. I couldn't risk trusting anyone, so I lied about my identity and about knowing him—just like Justin Smith had instructed me to do if ever I found myself is a situation like that."

Looking over at Captain Sanders, Mara said, "I saw you at the scene. I can't believe you found me here. Even weirder is the fact that I can't believe you know my mother. I'm not sure what's real anymore."

Capt. Jocelyn Sanders struggled to hide the glint of compassion that threatened to cross her face.

"I'm what's real, Mrs. Williams. I've known about you since Sergeant Smith first briefed me back in Homer. The fact that he's out of the picture is what brings me here to see you now."

Mara looked at the woman with interest.

"I don't blame you for not trusting the police, Mrs. Williams."

"Please, call me Mara."

"Okay then, Mara, I don't blame you for not trusting the police. I'm not saying there's anything funny going on there, but what I am saying is that the fewer lower-level officials who know every detail about this investigation, the better we're going to be at doing our job."

"But how can I be sure that I can trust you?" Mara asked.

"Faith," Jocelyn Sanders answered. "That's it. Faith. Maybe that's why we're fortunate that the talk we needed to have happened here today. Here, in front of Sal, who we both know is as good a judge of character as anyone I've ever met."

Mara stood and paced the room.

"You don't have a lot of options, Mara," Captain Sanders said. "You can choose to trust me or you can take your chances with everyone else, but on my friendship with Sal, here, I swear to you that I will do all I can to protect you and I'm asking you to trust me on that because, as weird as things have played out so far, they're likely to get a whole lot weirder before this is over."

Mara sat back down and reached for Sal's hand.

"The Stormy Maxwell I know isn't going to hurt one hair on your head, Mara," Sal said. "And even though I'm as shocked as anyone to learn that she's the law, I feel just as safe and at home with her now as if the last twenty years were all balled up into the time frame of yesterday."

Mara nodded.

"And don't forget that you've got me, too, Mara," Sal said. "And I'm not letting anything or anyone hurt you."

Chapter Thirty-One

What's Happening?

"I guess you probably know by now that I've got Anna out here on the *Storm Roamer* with me," Doug told Mara when they were finally able to talk over his satellite phone.

"Oh, no! Keep that Cory guy away from her!" she told him, but the signal was lost before she could fill him in either on the latest about Justin Smith or the break up between Anna and Cory.

Sal listened as Mara told her the news.

"I just saw Jocelyn Sanders at the grocery store and she said to tell you that your apartment is no longer available. She asked you to leave the key with the barista at the coffee shop—you know, the one you said sat with you after the shooting."

"That's weird, Sal, don't you think?"

"Nothing's weird to me anymore, Mara," Sal answered. "I'll take it down there for you if you want."

Mara removed the key from the pocket of her jeans and handed it to Sal.

"She also said to tell you that she knows about Anna and Cory, knows your relationship with Anna, and that it was she who sent Anna out to the *Storm Roamer* with Doug. Said Doug's been briefed. That's all I know."

Mara walked around the room, straightened a few things that really didn't need straightening, and then sat down.

"By the way, Della called earlier while you were in the shower. She said she's flying down here day after tomorrow. Said she's got something for you," Mara said.

"Now *that's* weird," Sal said.

When Della arrived two days later, both Mara and Sal were surprised to see how much weight she had lost, and that she had cut her long hair into a short bob.

"I needed less upkeep, you know?"

Both Sal and Mara commented on the new look, casting glances of confusion at each other when Della wasn't looking.

"It was my mom," Della said, as if reading their minds. "I just didn't have time for myself, you know?"

Mara excused herself and left the room, pretending to go to retrieve something. What was going on with Della anyway?

When she returned, she saw Della with her head lowered and with Sal's arm around her shoulders.

"Mom died last Monday," Della said.

"The funeral was last week," Sal said.

"Uncle Joe will understand that there wasn't time to call him," Sal told Della.

Mara felt tears well up. She had never really talked to Mary, but she knew from things that Joe had told her what a good woman she had been. She touched the quill bracelet that Mary had made for her and thought of the beaded moose hide medallion that Mary had also made for Thor. Those simple gifts spoke of a woman who gave more than she took. Of someone who used art and beauty to express who she was and of someone, who in spite of never having met her, had brought goodness and calmness into her Mara's own life.

"I'm sorry, Della," Mara said.

The three women sat together as Della explained the last few weeks. Mary had gone quickly after being diagnosed with cancer, and she had only suffered near the end during a time in which nurses came every day and administered the medications that temporarily dulled the pain.

"I didn't tell Uncle Joe because I knew he would take it too hard," Della said. "And I didn't tell him because I didn't want him to know that I took this."

Della reached into her pocket and handed Sal the feather with the red dot that Joe had been looking for so long.

"I know that stealing is wrong," she said. "But I thought it would help my mom. I wanted it to make her pain stop and make her feel peace, so I took it one night when Uncle Joe was taking a nap."

Della lowered her head and fell silent.

Mara said nothing and neither did Sal. Instead, both women walked to the sofa, each sitting beside Della and each placing an arm around the grieving girl who had endured so much pain herself. In the process, the feather fell and landed at their feet. For a moment it seemed that the red dot flickered in the light, but when Mara leaned to pick the it up, the dot was still solidly there. She handed the feather to Sal.

"You should be the one to tell him," she said, before leaning over to kiss Della gently on the cheek.

Chapter Thirty-Two

Into the Night

When Joe Michael flew into Hoonah that night, he pulled Mara's plane into the hangar and slid the door sideways, where it closed with a thump. He hadn't told anyone he was coming home. If he had, surely they would have tried to stop him. But Hoonah was his home and it had been his home since birth. There was no one who knew the area better than he did, and damned if anyone tried to get in the way of his need to return to this aboriginal place.

After unlocking the door to the house and making sure that everything was as it should be, he grabbed his shotgun and his sidearm, and then a bag of pistachios from the pantry, and another bag of salmon jerky, which he stuffed next to a single bottled water in his jacket pocket.

The skiff pushed easily into the water and slid silently into the night. Led only by the full moon, he drifted with the outgoing tide and then paddled silently over to Graveyard Island, where he beached the skiff—tying it to a tree for good measure—and climbed onto the rocky beach near the stand of totems that had been erected in memory of so many who had gone before.

When he reached the place where his own memorial totem supposedly had once stood, he found the ground covered in moss and spattered with spruce seedlings of various ages. Perhaps he had reached the wrong location, for it had been here last time he checked.

He walked around, trying to get his bearings, before tiring from the effort and sitting on a log to enjoy a snack. He awoke with the morning sun to find himself leaning against the very pole that had been erected to memorialize him. It was the same as he remembered, only a bit more weathered, but still strong.

He touched it all around its circumference and then up its sides as high as he could reach. It felt cold in the damp ocean air—and solid. The feather was still there, as was the red dot, now faded from years in the sun.

He smiled at how the feather reminded him of the very one he had carved in Sitka and chuckled out loud at the thought that he had possibly started some kind of trend. Then he took out his smartphone and took a couple of pictures before returning to his skiff and making his way across the water back to Hoonah.

He had been lucky to have chosen a time when the water lay flat and the winds had been still. He passed a couple of otters lolling in the morning sun and thought he saw a whale breach on the distant horizon.

When he reached Hoonah, he tied the skiff securely to another tree after pulling it up clear of the maximum high-tide line. He used two ropes—one in front and one behind—in case of high winds, and even laid some boards across its width for good measure. Then he walked home, unlocked the door and rustled up a good hearty breakfast, all the while wondering if last night had actually been the most realistic dream he could remember.

Chapter Thirty-Three

It Was Me

The next day when he called Sal, Joe didn't mention the trip to Graveyard Island except to say that he had decided to return to Hoonah and had taken the skiff out for a little run. He told himself that he needed to think about it all some more before telling her and that when he did tell her about it, he wanted it to be in person.

For her part, Sal expressed the expected displeasure at the fact that her husband might have placed himself in danger, then proceeded to tell him that Mary had died and that the funeral had taken place the previous week.

"Look, Joe, the point is that I miss you. Things sure are still up in the air around here, but I was thinking of flying over to Juneau for a couple of days to see you before you said you were back in Hoonah."

"I'm fine, Sal," he answered, "and right now Mara needs you more than I do."

"But, Joe—"

"Hang on, someone's at the door," he told her.

When he peeked out the window, Joe saw Della shivering outside and quickly let her in.

"It's Della," he told Sal. "I'll call you later."

Della had definitely lost weight, even in the few weeks since Joe had last seen her. And her hair was shorter.

Aside from those physical changes though, there was something else different about the woman who was known as his niece. For one thing, she didn't seem to want to look him in the eye, and for another, why was she fidgeting with her bracelet?

"She was sick a lot longer than I told you. And then she died—last week," Della began.

"At first she didn't even want to tell me, but I knew there was something.

Finally, when she couldn't eat much or really take care of herself, I decided to move back up there to be with her."

Then, Della looked squarely at Joe.

"It was good that I did, Uncle Joe. She really needed me. She made me promise not to tell you. She said you would worry—that it would remind you of losing Betty. So I promised her. That's why I didn't tell you."

Della looked down again, and began to fidget with her bracelet. For several long minutes she said nothing and neither did Joe.

When Della looked up again, her face was pale and drawn.

"I took it, Uncle Joe."

Joe Michael stared at the young woman he had guarded since birth. What could be upsetting her so?

"Look, niece, there is nothing you could do that would upset me, okay?"

Della squirmed in her seat and then got up and walked around the room before sitting down next to the uncle who had been her rock for most of her life.

"I took the feather, Uncle Joe. Look, I know it was wrong, but I did it for Mom. I wanted to help her. I didn't know what to do. I just figured it might help her."

"I imagine it did," Joe answered.

"But she died," Della replied.

"We're all going to die, Della. But you gave her hope, and peace—and you gave her love in her last hours. How could that not have helped her?"

"But you've been so upset—and Mara and Sal have needed it, and they've been so upset—and—and it was selfish. It was selfish of me to think only of my need for the feather."

"Tell me about Mary's last days," Joe said.

Della began to recount her time spent with Mary during the last weeks before she died. Her voice was soothing and reflective of the rhythmic and somewhat monotonic accent typical of Alaska Natives.

Joe thought of Mary as Della talked. Mary was his wife Betty's twin sister. Few beside Betty had ever known that he and Mary had dated in high school. Theirs had been the passionate love of youth and their breakup, when Joe left for Vietnam, had been equally profound.

Mary had written to him while he was in Nam, telling him that she was doing fine and shocking him with the news that she would be marrying his brother, Stu, very soon. *I'm pregnant,* she had written. *Stu is going to be a wonderful father.*

It hadn't been until years later, long after Joe had married Mary's sister, Betty and fathered five children with her, that Mary had told him the truth about Della. *I was pregnant before I married Stu and you were the only man that I had ever been with until my wedding night. You must promise me that neither Stu nor Della will ever know—not as long as I'm alive,* and Joe had made that promise because he knew it meant so much to Mary.

Over the course of their marriage, Betty had often made the observation that Joe hadn't been the same in the days and years after returning from Vietnam, and she chalked that up to the war. For his part, Joe never came to terms with the secret he had bound himself to carry— not just the secret, but the fact that he never told Betty what her sister had shared.

When Betty and their children all died in the house fire accidentally started by Stu, Joe decided that it was punishment for his silence. Guilty about keeping the secret he had pledged to keep to Mary, he had refused to blame his brother for the accident, and instead blamed himself. After all, if not for the burden of the secret, none of this would be happening. None of this tragic, destructive, overwhelming, chaotic pain would have befallen him.

It was then that he had started riding the ferry and it was then that he basically withdrew from the human race. Not until meeting Mara and handing her the feather had he cared enough to live again.

Now both Mary and Betty were gone. Stu was gone now, too. Della was all who was left of his original life and she was here in Hoonah now throwing herself at his mercy over the taking of a feather that he would so gladly have given her, if only he had known how much she wanted it.

Maybe that is why he had not let Sal come back. All of this preceded his life with Sal and even his life with Mara, whose father he had saved in Vietnam, and he needed time alone.

He was quick in making the decision as he felt the burden of a lifetime of secrecy lift from his heart.

"Della, sit down here. There is something we need to talk about."

Chapter Thirty-Four

Escape

The sound was deafening, causing Della to drop her cup of coffee on the floor and sending Joe Michael reaching for his shotgun. A second explosion, much louder than the first, quickly followed, and then a huge fireball rose above the trees near the docks.

"Let's go, Della!" Joe yelled, racing for the hangar.

Joe pushed the door to the hangar open and with Della's help, pushed the plane out into the yard.

"Get in!" he hollered.

It was all the old man could do to move quickly enough to get the Cessna airborne, but somehow he reached tree top level before seeing two men run out of the woods, spread gasoline around his cabin, and ignite it.

He grabbed the satellite phone that he always kept in the plane and dialed Sal.

"They just blew up the dock and torched the cabin. Tell that cop woman. Della and I are on our way to Juneau."

By the time they landed in Juneau, the pain in Joe's chest was crushing and he was having trouble drawing a deep breath. He handed the phone to Della.

"Call 911 . . ."

By the time Sal got the call from Della, Joe Michael had already been evaluated, rushed into surgery and had two stents placed in his coronary arteries. And, by the time Della had finished telling both Sal and Mara that the home in Hoonah had been set on fire, Jocelyn Sanders herself was on a plane to Hoonah along with Sgt. Larry Allen Kenton, who was already in the process of returning from California.

"Did you get a hold of Sal?" Joe Michael asked Della when he returned to the Coronary Care Unit from surgery.

"I talked to her twice," Della answered. "The woman FBI agent is on her way to Hoonah. So is some other guy who was in California."

Joe Michael was white as the sheets he lay on, but he felt better than he had hours earlier. An IV line was running fluid into his right arm, and he had a sandbag on his right groin area that the nurse had told him was there to help seal up the hole where they had accessed his arteries to insert the stent. Della stroked his arm and then gently tucked the feather under his hand where Joe was able to feel it against the sheets.

"You're lucky we got it when we did," the surgeon said, walking up to Joe and brushing past Della as he did. "Another month or so and—well, things went well, Mr. Michael, and you should be fine and ready to go home by tomorrow."

Joe closed his eyes and went to sleep with the image of the fireball and the two men igniting his cabin pushed out of his consciousness by the sedation the nurse had just given him.

When he awoke the next morning, Della was sitting by his bed, as were Jocelyn Sanders and Larry Allen Kenton.

"Do you have anything else you'd like to add to your story, Della?" Jocelyn asked.

"No. I told you everything," Della replied.

"My men found this in the yard near the hangar," Jocelyn Sanders said.

Joe lifted his head as Captain Sanders held up a baggie with a gray scarf bearing the orange image of a volcano in the corner.

"Mr. Michael, we're dealing with something much bigger and more sinister than we first imagined.

"That's why we're going to assign bodyguards to you, Mara, and Sal. Della has refused them," she continued. "Sergeant Kenton here will brief you."

With that ominous statement, Captain Sanders turned and walked out of the room—the only sound being the click, click, click, of her sensible heels.

Chapter Thirty-Five

Juneau

S al and Mara arrived at the Juneau airport just as Joe Michael was being wheeled out of the side door of the hospital to a waiting cab. Supposedly, Della had cleaned the Juneau cabin and left something for him to eat before leaving to return to Glenallen.

With the feather tucked into his breast pocket, Joe Michael lifted himself from the wheelchair and climbed into the cab, leaning forward briefly to tell the driver his destination.

It had all been as simple as that. One day walking across the kitchen in Hoonah before suddenly having to fly for his life away from the island of his birth, and the next day waking up in the Coronary Care unit of a Juneau hospital with IVs sticking out of both arms.

While Sal took a cab to the cabin, Mara stayed behind to check on the plane and pay any storage fees.

"You two need some time alone," she had told Sal.

The old woman had agreed, reasoning that she and Mara had been seen in Dutch Harbor, Mara had discovered Anna there, and Sal herself had made contact with several of the old-timers she had known during her time living in Alaska.

"I just told 'em we was out on a run," she had whispered to Mara on the plane carrying them back to Juneau. "Left everthin' out like we was still there and told ma buddy that owns the cabin we been usin' to keep a watch out on our stuff and that we'd be back in about a week."

Thor hadn't enjoyed flying in cargo on the way back and had let Mara know about that by refusing to come when she called him for the first hour off the plane. Eventually he got over it enough to let her give him water and some special rubs on his neck and so while Sal headed to see her husband, Mara let Thor roam the grounds of the small airport her plane had been towed to.

"He knows to stay back," she told both the airport guard and the undercover agent who had been assigned to her.

"It's my mother you'd better watch out for," she laughed, directing her comment to the bodyguard the FBI had provided. "Haven't found anyone who can corral her yet."

Sal got out of the taxi and walked past the first eight cabins on the boardwalk to get home. When she passed the one belonging to Doug and Mara, she jiggled the doorknob just for the heck of it and found that all was secure; then she dragged her suitcase past the next cabin, paused to look over the railing into the harbor water, and gently turned the knob.

Joe Michael was sitting back in his recliner with his eyes closed, but opened them long enough to see that Sal had returned before closing them again.

"They told me what happened," she said as she wheeled her suitcase into the bedroom. "There was no way I could have gotten here in time. Thank god for Della."

Joe Michael did not respond, so Sal spent the next fifteen minutes unpacking her bag and let him rest. When she walked back into the living room, she saw the feather tucked under her husband's softly folded hands.

"Mara's at the airport—and Thor. Checking on the plane."

Still Joe Michael said nothing.

"I was sick when I heard," she said, "but not as sick as I was thinking I might lose you."

A tear trickled down Joe Michael's cheek as he opened his eyes and pushed the control that slowly raised the recliner.

"There was an explosion. Then they burned the house," he said, visibly shaken.

"I know," Sal said.

Joe Michael closed his eyes again and heaved several deep sighs.

"I see that Della gave you the feather," Sal said, redirecting the conversation.

"I learned she had it right before she flew to Hoonah, but to spare Della, I didn't want to tell you until I could tell you to your face."

"She told me about Mary," Joe answered. "And now I need to tell you a couple of things."

"They don't matter, sweet baby. Whatever they are they don't matter. Right now you need to rest and so do I. How about I make us something to eat and we go to bed? You can tell me tomorrow, okay?"

Chapter Thirty-Six

New Reality

Sal hugged Joe after he told her about Della, feeling his shoulders relax and hearing a sigh from his lips when she did. There wasn't much to say at a moment like this, a moment when someone has summoned the courage to reveal a tightly held life's secret, but she tried.

"You must feel so free," she said. "Like the way I felt with Mara."

Joe Michael tightened the grip on his wife's hand and pulled her closer. Sal sank into his arms as the two stood rocking gently in the silence of their embrace. The sound of engines broke the mood as both turned to see a fleet of seiners heading out of the harbor.

"I've always loved this place," Sal said. "So peaceful, but yet so energizing."

Joe didn't answer. The cabin had belonged to his brother, Stu, before he died, and served as yet another example of the way the lives of the two brothers had been entwined. For Joe, the remembrance of the two men pouring gasoline on his own cabin as he flew off overtook him as a wave of sadness took the color from his face.

"I think I'll sit down for a minute," he said, before looking at Sal and saying, "I'm glad we have this place, too."

Minutes later, Mara arrived with Thor.

"Everything looks fine with the plane. I paid for a hangar for now—until we find out more, you know, about the house in Hoonah."

Joe Michael got up and walked to the bedroom.

"I'm gonna take a nap now."

Mara said nothing as she watched the old man shuffle across the room with Sal right behind him making sure that everything was okay.

It was as if a piece of himself had died with the Hoonah cabin, or could she have just misread his demeanor? After all, he had just suffered a heart attack after enduring an experience that some half his age would have had trouble coping with.

When Sal came back out, the two nodded as Mara picked up her things and called Thor to her.

"I'm going to go get groceries. I'll bring you some basics, okay?"

"Okay," Sal answered.

Sal watched her daughter walk along the boardwalk to her own cabin, and then come back out with a purse and a cell phone in her hand. She watched her call Thor to her and let him into the back door of her SUV, then walk around and climb inside herself. Then she watched her start the vehicle, look at her makeup in the rear view mirror and then drive off.

She took a broom from behind the door and began sweeping the wooden slats in front of their cabin, stopping to watch a sea lion swim up alongside some smaller boats before diving and reappearing several feet away. Then she shook out the doormat, straightened it and put it back in place before shutting the door, pulling the shades, and climbing into bed next to her husband.

She was long asleep before Joe Michael, too, fell into restful slumber, but he did, right there beside his wife, who represented the only security he knew right then. When the feather fell from his hand, it fluttered down to the floor, landing inside one of his slippers, where it stayed while he slept.

In a few short hours, he would wake to the aroma of dinner being prepared by Sal's daughter, and he would begin life in the world of his new reality.

Chapter Thirty-Seven

Gone! Everything!

Despite repeated protests from both Sal and Mara, Joe Michael insisted on traveling with them to Hoonah. The next morning, the three of them and Thor as well as a trio of assigned bodyguards flew into Hoonah on a plane chartered by the FBI.

Mara insisted on personally driving Joe Michael to the home site, using a spare SUV she and Doug kept at the airport in Hoonah.

The scene they arrived at was worse than they could have imagined. Joe and Sal's cabin was burned to the ground and the hangar/shop was mostly burned, with a section of roof hanging precariously over a few remaining steel support beams. Yellow police tape surrounded the place where both buildings had stood, reminding the group that they were not to disturb anything.

"I need to see the dock area," Joe said after scanning what remained of his beloved home. "That's where the first explosion came from."

When they got there, all three wished that they hadn't. Although the *Beachmopper* was still afloat, a large charred area of melted metal now occupied her deck and the door to the pilothouse was creaking loudly as it swung on one remaining hinge in the wind. Amazingly, though, Joe's skiff was still tied to the trees and appeared undisturbed.

With the help of the three security agents, they untied it and pulled it into the water. Joe Michael climbed inside, followed by Sal, Mara and one agent. Silently they motored across the channel to Graveyard Island, where Joe was the first to climb out, followed by the others. Together they beached the skiff and walked up the wide gravel beach to the line of totems that had stood in this spot for decades.

Nothing had changed in this place that stood as an oasis in time. No one said much of anything as they stood there surrounded by the massive memorials to those who had gone before. An aura of peace enveloped each of them as fog rolled in with the lap of each wave, cloaking the island with misty comfort—the rumble of the gently tumbling beach rocks the only sound.

After a respectful pause, they climbed back into the skiff and headed back to Hoonah.

Sal was the first to spot three humpbacks swimming near the shore, but soon enough, everyone had fixed their eyes on the beautiful and peaceful scene of the whales swimming along in the pristine green Alaskan waters.

The sound of them spouting water through their dual blowholes seemed to harmonize with the gentle splash of their backs rising and falling in the still waters of the bay. The whales had come up close to the skiff, but despite their giant size, had not caused even a ripple of disruption to the safety of the four.

"It's as if they're guiding us," Mara whispered.

And so they did, swimming for several minutes alongside the tiny raft before gliding forward and taking a deep dive, leaving the magnificent sight of their massive tails dripping a waterfall of sparkling ocean for the instant before they were gone.

Joe Michael took a deep breath and then another. It was as if he wanted to inhale every ounce of the purity of this place. He sat for a moment and took it all in, before lifting his oars from the water and reaching back to start the engine to the skiff. As the small group sped back to Hoonah immersed in their own private thoughts, Joe Michael straightened his shoulders, awash in new resolve and in the determination to rebuild his home in the place of his birth.

If it took the rest of his life and the last breath he would draw, he would rebuild. He would do it for Sal, for Mara, and for the woman who still did not know she was his daughter, Della, but most importantly, he would do it for himself. It was who he was, it was how he rolled, and it was how it was going to be.

Chapter Thirty-Eight

Phone Reassurance—
If You Can Call It That

Jocelyn Sanders called Mara the next morning to say she had been in touch with Doug and had told him what had happened with Joe. Even though Joe was doing well, he and Sal had agreed that he should go to Sitka to stay with his friend, John, just so that he would not be alone.

"They've got a good hospital there if you need it," Sal had reasoned, "and you and John need to firm up the totem ceremony details anyway."

Meanwhile, Sal and Mara had decided to return to Dutch Harbor, mostly to satisfy Sal's desire to reconnect with the fishing community there in hopes of finding some clue as to why Mara and Doug—and now Joe Michael and herself— were being targeted by those she referred to as "those danged nasty, too-rotten-even-fer-bait little perps."

Before they left, Jocelyn Sanders arranged a phone call between Mara and Doug.

"Anna's safe with me," Doug told her. "It's just the two of us on the *Storm Roamer*—you know, besides our deckhand."

"Is she doing okay?" Mara asked.

"She's fine," Doug answered. "Hamlet and I are keeping her plenty busy here."

"What's with this Hamlet guy?" Mara asked.

"Just a crew member sent by Jocelyn Sanders, Mara. Forty-something black guy who says he's out of Seattle. Kind of keeps to himself. Does his job. Doesn't say much."

"What about Cory? Is Anna safe from Cory?"

"He's on the *Driftfeather* with Derrk , Joey, and a guy named J.D. who I haven't met. Jocelyn sent him too. Don't worry, we're plenty safe," he said, hoping that his voice sounded convincing.

The truth was that he wasn't all that sure that they were safe, considering everything that had gone on, but he had always subscribed to the "build it and they will come" theory of life, and so he figured that if he acted safe, and told himself they were safe, that somehow they would *be* safe.

He tried not to think of that day in the garage, or of his own kidnapping when he did, just as he tried not to think of the danger that his wife was in or the difficulty he was having in quelling his anger over the burning of Joe and Sal's Hoonah home and business.

Nor did he allow memories of the previous destruction of his first seiner, the *Fire Ring Roamer,* or the long journey he had taken in deciding to purchase his current seiner, the *Storm Roamer,* cloud his mind.

Doug Williams had learned long ago that a clouded mind serves no purpose other than to confuse the present, and so he ratcheted his thinking into the positive mode and the productive and rational mode, just as he had done on countless other occasions starting with the death of his brother, Dan.

The seas were calm right now and he took advantage of that to take a short nap, turning operation of the *Storm Roamer* over to Hamlet.

For her part, Anna had busied herself in the galley— a sure sign that they would be eating well tonight. It was amazing to see the woman she had become. Mara had no reason to worry about his brother's daughter or her ability to manage herself. For a moment, he was sorry that neither Dan nor Mara could be here to observe the other side of Anna, who few besides himself had been privileged to see.

He felt the anger rise inside just as it always did when he thought of Dan and how his life had ended prematurely just as he felt the amazement that always rose when recalling that he had met Mara because it had.

"In due time," he whispered as he dozed off. "She'll find out when she's supposed to."

Chapter Thirty-Nine

Staying Low

When Mara and Sal arrived back in Dutch Harbor, they did so with a determination to once and for all confront the danger that had created such havoc with their lives. Thor was with them, of course. Mara would never board him or leave him with strangers.

The dog had long ago learned to travel well and to keep his presence well integrated with his owners. Few ever saw Mara without her dog at her side, just as few ever saw the animal bark or create any kind of disturbance. So when Mara and Thor caught the attention of two guys wearing dark hoodies walking along the harbor, they quickly disappeared among the boats, even taking the unusual step of boarding one temporarily to make it seem that they were there on business.

Fortunately, the plan worked and the two suspicious-looking young men soon moved on.

"That was close," Mara said, stroking Thor's head, before walking back up to the walkway—first meandering through town, and then heading to their temporary home.

It wasn't unusual to see people with their dogs in Alaska—especially big dogs like Thor. And it was easy for Mara to blend in with the many other women who dressed in baggy jackets, canvas pants, and rubber boots as they worked in fishing-related endeavors. Still, she knew that she needed to be careful. Something was going on, and until she and the others knew just what that something was, she would need to keep a clear eye out for danger.

Sal wasn't home when she got back to their cabin, so Mara fixed herself a sandwich and shared the last bite with Thor.

They had just settled in front of the woodstove when suddenly Thor jumped up and bolted out the door that Mara always left loosely closed in case he needed to go out.

When she got to the window, she could see him lunging across the yard before disappearing into the woods behind the house. Before she could grab her coat and her gun, a shot rang out and then another. She heard a yelp.

"Thor!" she screamed. "Thor!"

She felt her heart racing and tried to suppress the lump in her throat that was threatening to steal her breath.

"Oh my ...," she said as she ran, pushing her bodyguard aside as she bolted out the door. "Thor! Thor!"

In the distance she could hear the sound of breaking branches and the thump of footsteps running away from her. Then silence.

With tears streaming down her face, she followed Thor's tracks into the woods. After going about 100 yards, she saw the first drops of blood, then larger pools of blood scattered along the way.

Nearly blinded by tears, she moved forward, her gun drawn just in case, with the silence now overwhelming all else within earshot.

What was the heaviness in her chest?

She sat down on a fallen tree and tried to catch her breath, but jumped up when she heard a rustle in the brush behind her. Thankfully it was her bodyguard, who slipped past her and started making his way up the trail.

It was a good ten minutes before he returned, and when he did, he found Mara still sitting on the stump with a panting Thor by her side.

"There's a little blood around his muzzle," she said. "He must have got one of them . . ."

The guard took out a small test kit and took a swab of the blood around Thor's mouth, hesitant at first, in case the dog reacted in a negative way, but Thor was cooperative with the process—seeming to understand what was happening.

"We'll run some tests on this," the guard said.

When he was done, Mara opened Thor's mouth and looked for any sign of injury. There was none.

"It does seem like he got hold of one of them," she said.

"I found this on the trail, too," the guard said, holding up a handgun wrapped in one of the Baggies he always carried in his pocket. "And this scarf."

Mara felt the blood drain from her face when she saw the gray bandana with the orange volcano image in one corner.

"From now on, you don't move unless I tell you to move, Mrs. Williams. Understood?"

Chapter Forty

Perps in Custody

M ara sat across the table from Sal in the cabin while their two
bodyguards huddled over their cellphone in the living room.
As the two women sat there silently looking out the window, they
could hear snippets of conversation coming from the other room.

" . . . bad shot . . . same bandana . . . yeah . . . dog got one of 'em . . ."

"Yes, Captain Sanders. Right away. Affirmative."

Sal was the first to break the silence between the two women.

"Hell's afire already, Mara!"

Mara reached across the table and placed her hand over her mother's.
Even though Sal had retained the same crusty demeanor that she had
always known her for, the unveiling of her true identity as both Sylvia
La Monte and as her birth mother had somehow softened the hearty
edge that had protected the old woman for so long.

"If I know Jocelyn Sanders like I think I do . . ." Sal began.

"I'm sorry to interrupt, Mrs. Michael," one of the agents said, "but I
thought you'd want to know that Unalaska PD just picked up the two
suspects who we believe posed a threat to Mrs. Williams."

"Sorry piece's-a-scat!" Sal exclaimed.

"Seems that one of them turned up in the ER at the clinic with a bite wound to the calf. We're checking now to see if his blood matches up with what we found around Thor's mouth."

"What about Thor?" Mara asked.

"Not to worry, Mrs. Williams. It was a clear case of defense and his rabies immunization is current, so not to worry."

"Matter of fact," the other agent said, "we're probably going to put him in for a heroism award once all this settles down."

Mara smiled. If it came about, this wouldn't be Thor's first heroism award for sure. Even now, at the age of 7 years, Thor was still the wonderful companion he had always been.

"They're getting ready to ship the guy up to Anchorage," the first agent said. "Something about infection and blood supply from constriction . . . not quite sure."

"And don't worry about his accomplice," the second agent said. "He's in custody and we're hoping we can get some information out of him before he gets transferred to the jail in Kodiak."

Chapter Forty-One

FBI On Board

"You make a pretty good dinner omelet for a rookie FBI agent, Miss Williams," Hamlet said to Anna.

"And you make a pretty good weirdo deck hand for an undercover FBI agent," Anna replied.

Hamlet smiled and continued eating while Anna tidied up the galley.

"I'm not sure you'd be on this dangerous an operation if your uncle hadn't talked to Captain Sanders and convinced her that you would be the last person anyone would consider to be a cop."

Anna continued cleaning and said nothing, silently vowing to make Hamlet and every other seasoned member of law enforcement one day understand that her commitment to fighting crime and injustice was deeply implanted into the same heart that had nearly lost its will to beat after the death of her father.

"He's paying his own price for the risk," she said out loud. "My uncle . . ."

"How's that?" Hamlet said as he made a motion with one hand requesting some more toast.

"Keeping all this from my Aunt Mara is killing him."

This time Hamlet said nothing. How could someone like him relate to something like that? His first three marriages had all ended in divorce and his current wife was in the process of clearing everything they owned out of their house before she filed for what would be the fourth.

"Yeah, some guys get all that way over a woman," he said, trying harder than he should to sound detached. "Then there's guys like me that do what they want, when they want, where they want without lettin' some woman hold 'em back . . ."

Hamlet got up and carried his empty dish to the sink.

"You have yourself a good evening now, Agent Williams."

Anna stifled a smile. Hamlet was as transparent as any man she had ever met and as devastated at the failure of his relationships as a gentle soul like him could be. The truth was, in his line of work, long hours, lengthy travel, and the frequent need to go undercover were enough to undo all but the rarest of marriages.

It would probably be the same for her, she figured. Not that she had married anyone to test that theory yet. But it probably would be. She had resigned herself to that and then put it out of her mind, because as futile as her hope for eternal happiness seemed, she still longed for a wedding by the river up Knik River Rd., just like the one that had brought her mother and Ben together, and that also had sealed the love between Doug and Mara.

"Did I catch you daydreaming again?" Doug said from the doorway.

"Just thinking," Anna answered. "Did you have a good nap?"

Doug scratched his head and then eased into the booth beside the galley, where he sipped the hot coffee that Anna brought to him.

"Yeah. Pretty good."

Anna cracked a couple of eggs into a hot pan, then scrambled them just the way her uncle liked them.

"Your dad liked 'em that way, too," Doug said.

"I know," Anna answered.

Then, hiding the tears that had formed at the mention of her father she turned to her uncle and teased, "It's not like you're not brothers or something . . ."

Doug nodded, then bit into his toast.

"Well, brothers is what we were for sure, and brothers we'll stay, even if I have to do the job for both Dan and myself now that he's gone. Hey! How 'bout your mom and Ben," he asked, referring to his brother's widow, who by some weird twist of fate was now married to Mara's ex father-in-law.

"I wrote to them yesterday," Anna answered, "And gave the letter to Jocelyn who said she'd make sure it got mailed from the dorm at UAF in Fairbanks."

"I'm sure you told them that you're studying hard, huh?" Doug said wryly.

"I did my best," Anna replied.

Chapter Forty-Two

Pensiveness

Joe Michael left his fourth voicemail for Della. Why wasn't she answering his calls? He had been so close to telling her that he was her real father before she left, but the right moment had escaped him and he wasn't sure when it would present itself again. Besides, he had had second thoughts about telling her. What would it prove? He and Sal had already left everything they had to her in their will, so she would find out soon enough then, but meanwhile, for now, why complicate her life even more—especially so soon after her mother had died.

"You seem troubled, my friend," John, said.

Joe Michael looked up into the eyes of his lifetime friend and bared the hint of a smile, but said nothing.

"Let's check the totem," John said.

The two men walked to the carving center near Totem Park in Sitka and stood next to the cedar pole that John's son was in the process of finishing. Both men walked around the totem, examining every inch of the masterfully carved memorial, including the now restored feather with the red dot that Joe had finished working on that morning.

"It's as fine as any I've seen," John said, placing one hand on his son's shoulder and the other on Joe's.

Joe ran his hand lightly over the feather that he had painstakingly carved and painted, and then had carved and painted again. Although it had been as close to perfect the first time he had done it, it was even more so now. Whether it was because of the need for extra smoothing and deeper cuts that made the feather seem more powerful in its presence on the totem now or just his own emotional investment in the process was unclear, but the feather spoke to him in a way that left him fighting back tears of pride at the work, and so he took a moment to hold his hand against the ancient wood and feel its powerful energy come through the carving and into his hand.

John seemed to understand and chose to say nothing, instead standing shoulder to shoulder with the man who had been his friend since childhood. Together they stood under the overhang where the totem lay sideways, propped on a series of hollowed-out wood supports, and watched John's son continue to put the final touches on the pole.

"I suppose we should store these somewhere," Joe Michael said to both John and his son as he held up an old coffee can that contained the special paints he had mixed.

When no one answered, he walked out from under the overhang and across a small section of manicured lawn into the stand of spruce that held so many totems in this place called Totem Park in Sitka, Alaska.

As a light drizzle fell through the forest onto all that was below, he made his way across the winding paths to the outer edge of the park, stepping over several of the giant slugs that inhabited the area as he did. Then he stepped off the trail and made his way down a small embankment, found a hollowed-out fallen tree about halfway down, and shoved the can deep inside, using care to make sure that the plastic lid remained tightly secured and that the can remained upright. He then covered the area with branches and leaves in a way that left the area looking undisturbed to all but himself, placing a special marker on a nearby tree just in case he needed to find the paints again.

He gave no thought to the possibility that he might slip on the sedges and moss that covered the area, nor did he pay any mind to the potential that a bear could be nearby. He had spent a lifetime walking among the great bears of Alaska and had experienced more peaceful encounters than not. Although conscious of potential threats to his safety, and always carrying a firearm just in case, he did as he had always done and walked the woodlands in peace, grateful when that peace was returned to him yet another time.

Then he walked out of the dense forest and into life once more— alone with his thoughts, alone with his plan for life, and as he had come into this world, alone.

Chapter Forty-Three

Got a Hunch

" *Storm Roamer*, this is the *Driftfeather*, come in."

"*Driftfeather*, go ahead," Anna said into the mike with more trepidation than she had anticipated.

It was clearly Cory's voice on the mike, but somehow he hadn't seemed to recognize hers. Maybe it was because she had used the official on-duty voice that those in law enforcement have perfected, or perhaps he had failed to make the connection. Whatever the case, she liked that he didn't know who he was talking to.

The two seiners had been fishing in the surrounding waters since their arrival while they waited for the weather in the Bering Sea to clear and by all estimates, would be coming into Dutch Harbor that night before heading out at first light to the fishing grounds.

"Captain Derrk says we're gonna move on ahead and hit Dutch this afternoon. Will connect with you tonight," Cory said.

"Affirmative, *Driftfeather*," Anna answered. "Will check with you on our arrival."

"Could be something coming down," Hamlet told Anna and Doug after Anna shared the news. "I'm guessing they did some kind of intercept out on the water and are bringing a delivery in along with their fish this afternoon."

"It's not cast in stone," he added. "It's just a hunch. Interesting, though, that a deckhand made the call."

By now the *Storm Roamer* was close enough in for Doug to get ahold of Mara by phone. Weird that she wasn't answering. He left a message saying they would be in around dusk and left it at that. He had long ago gotten used to lapses in their communication and when he had talked to her a few days ago, all had been fine.

As the three lingered over dinner in relatively calm seas, they talked about how they would handle the trip ashore, including allotting enough time to offload the fish and secure the *Storm Roamer* before settling in for the night.

They agreed that Doug would go find Sal and Mara under the assumption that he wouldn't be recognized in the darkness that would have fallen by then. They also agreed that Anna would remain on board the seiner and that Hamlet would go into town for supplies. This, they figured, would create the most natural effect and not arouse suspicion on the off chance that they were being watched.

By the time they reached the docks, it was already dark, but Doug could see the *Driftfeather* tied up alongside several other seiners in the harbor.

While he proceeded to oversee the offloading of the fish, across town his wife, Mara, was pacing nervously outside the apartment she had once rented.

"She's a lot more 'n a barista if ya ask me," Sal barked.

Mara looked at her quizzically.

"I'm jest sayin' that she was awful secretive about lettin' any more 'n one a ma fingers in that door," Sal said. "And that was even after I reminded her that we had met after the shooting of Justin Smith."

"Well, at least you gave her the key," Mara answered, "and so we don't have to deal with her anymore."

The two women walked along the boardwalk beside the harbor as Thor sniffed a few feet ahead of them. About halfway along the waterfront, they ran into Doug and Hamlet, with both Doug and Mara playing it cool so as not to let on that they knew each other.

"Yeah, see ya, man," Doug called as Hamlet moved on toward town and Doug pretended to move across the street away from the women.

When the coast was clear, Mara ran into his arms, and the two shared a lingering embrace.

"Don't take no brains fer me to know I need ta get lost," Sal said. "Howzabout if I meet ya for breakfast down at Amelia's about eleven tomorrow. That work?"

Sal winked at Doug, who winked back.

"Make that six and we've got a date," he said. "Need to be pulling out to sea by eight."

"I'll be in town here visitin' a coupla ma old friends," Sal said.

"We'll be at the cabin then," Mara answered.

Doug and Mara waited to make sure that Sal got to her destination safely, then they spent the next two hours walking around Dutch Harbor while Doug filled her in on everything he knew about their apparent mission out at sea.

"I just found out about Anna being in the FBI myself," he told her, "but she's as professional as it gets when you see her in action. You'd feel proud."

He also talked about Hamlet being an undercover federal agent and that as far as he was concerned, any further encounters between them would be as strangers and with her using her alias of Alisa Allison.

By the time the two of them got back to the cabin, had fed Thor and themselves, it was midnight, but they remained wide awake, spending more time than usual savoring each other before falling asleep around three.

When Thor woke them up at five, it seemed as if they had both just fallen asleep, and the temptation to remain in bed felt close to overpowering.

"There's not a minute that goes by that I don't think of moments like this with you," Doug told his wife. "Which makes it so hard to leave again right now."

Mara didn't resist when he pulled her to him again and she didn't let him see her tears when she watched him walk down the path away from the cabin an hour later.

"C'mon, Thor," she said. "Let's catch a couple more hours sleep, okay?"

Chapter Forty-Four

Ambushed

"They've got Anna," Hamlet said as Doug crawled onto the seiner. "They left this note."

SHOULDA NEVER LEFT HER ALONE LIKE THIS, CAPTAIN WILLIAMS. NOW YOU'RE GOING TO HAVE TO SPEND A LITTLE EFFORT TRACKING YOUR LITTLE NIECE DOWN. IT'S KIND OF LIKE DÉJÀ VU, ISN'T IT, CAP-TAIN? MAYBE A LITTLE REMEMBRANCE OF THAT TIME IN TALKEETNA A FEW YEARS BACK WHEN YOU THOUGHT YOU COULD SAVE YOUR BROTHER. DON'T WORRY, THOUGH, WE WON'T HARM YOUR NIECE, WHY THAT WOULD BE JUST WAY TOO EERIE NOW, WOULDN'T IT?

"I've already contacted Jocelyn Sanders," Hamlet said. "How'd they know she was alone on that boat last night? It's not like I saw anyone except for Derrk, Joey, and his deckhand—you know, Cory."

When Doug saw the gray scarf tied to the wheelhouse door, it was all he could do to fight back one of the headaches that had plagued him since he had been abducted.

"How about we put that in a Baggie or something and not touch it," Hamlet said, grasping the scarf with fingers that were covered with the outside of the Baggie and then securing it safely inside.

"I need to tell Mara—warn Mara," Doug said.

He dialed her before Hamlet could stop him, telling her that Anna was gone and about the scarf.

"I've got more bad news," Mara said, "Derrk just came by and said that Cory is gone, too. If he hurts her, Doug . . ."

Before Mara could finish her conversation with her husband, Sal was out the door, grabbing a canvas jacket on her way out.

"Stay put, Mara. Keep Thor close to you. Load your gun and keep it nearby. Jocelyn Sanders is sending your bodyguard back. Said it was a mistake to pull him off duty like she did yesterday. Same guy. Watch for him and let him in when you see him."

"What about you, Sal?" Mara said, knowing that the fact that Sal had reverted to her base dialect meant that this was serious.

"I'll be fine. Danged bodyguards were crampin' my style anyway."

"Thor and I are right behind you," Mara called. "I'm not sitting here waiting for anyone."

Mara didn't see the hint of a smile that crossed her mother's lips, nor did she see which direction Sal had taken at the blind corner down from the cabin.

By the time Jocelyn Sanders and her men arrived, both women were long gone, leaving Captain Sanders with no choice but to set up temporary headquarters inside the cabin until she could get her plan B organized in her head.

After confirming with Doug that Hamlet was on the *Storm Roamer* with him and that Derrk and his deckhand, J.D., were on board the *Driftfeather* she contacted the harbormaster's office to make sure that both vessels' mooring costs were taken care of indefinitely, with all charges going to the US Department of Homeland Security.

When Jocelyn Sanders summoned Doug to the cabin, he was reluctant to go. What if it were some kind of a trap? He went, though. Anything was better than sitting on that boat waiting for some kind of news.

"Thank you for coming, Mr. Williams," Jocelyn Sanders said. "I know how difficult all this must be for you, especially—"

"Look, with all due respect, Captain Sanders, cut the crap, okay. I've been through enough drama in the last five years to fill twelve crime logs, so please stop patronizing me and tell me what is going on here!"

As unlike Doug Williams as it was for him to behave this way, he was worried sick about his wife, his niece, his seiners and crew, and even about himself. The headache was excruciating. The doctors had called them posttraumatic migraines—whatever that meant. Were they from stress? The whack on his head? Worry? All three?

"Your niece is safe, Mr. Williams, but you're the only one besides law enforcement that can know that, and I'm only telling you because of your obvious suffering—and maybe because I'm going soft in my old age."

Doug Williams dropped to a chair.

"Your wife is safe, too. I know you need to know that. She doesn't know it, but I've got three bodyguards on her, her phone is being monitored, and most of her moves are being recorded."

Doug tried to stand, but the headache forced him back into the chair.

"It's not that we think she did anything," Jocelyn Sanders said. "Matter of fact, we know that she's as much a victim as you are. But we have our reasons and unfortunately I am not at liberty to share them with you."

"Well, I'm at liberty to share this with *you,*" Doug said, raising one fist and trying to stand.

"Why don't you just sit back down, son, and let Captain Sanders here do her job," Larry Allen Kenton said from the doorway.

"Stovepipe?" Doug said.

"That's right, now, son. That's how you know me."

"But your leg, it's—it's not gone."

"It's a long story, son, and there's gonna be plenty of time for me to explain it to you back at the shop in Kenai."

"Hell there is!" Doug said standing again.

"Sit down, Mr. Williams," Jocelyn Sanders said. "You're not going anywhere except back to the garage with Sergeant Kenton here."

Chapter Forty-Five

Miffed

D oug Williams did not like this turn of events any more than he liked knowing that his wife and niece were out there and under the supposed protection of a bunch of cops that had suddenly decided to take over his life.

He went peacefully with Sergeant Kenton, though, because in his mind to not do so might have placed them in even more danger.

"Look, I know this makes no sense, man," Sergeant Kenton said.

"No more sense than the sudden reappearance of your leg," Doug shot back.

"Don't blame you for the sarcasm," Sergeant Kenton said. "I'd be the same way, but by now you know that I'm a cop and I know you're smart enough to have figured out that the garage is a cover for both covert operations and witness protection."

"So which am I?" Doug snapped. "The covert operation or the protected witness?"

"Again, I understand your frustration, Mr. Williams, just as I understand how hard it is for you to trust me right now."

Doug reached for his head. The conversation with Sergeant Kenton had done nothing to ease his headache. In fact, it had made it worse. Maybe it *was* a migraine.

"If anything happens to my wife, or my niece—I swear to god—if one hair on either of their heads—hear what I'm saying?" Doug told Kenton.

"I'm gonna have to blindfold you now," Sergeant Kenton said. "We need to get you moved to the garage and for your own safety, I can't let you know where it is or how you got there."

"Why don't you mothers just drug me?" Doug snarled.

Doug barely had the words out of his mouth before someone reached from behind and tied his arms behind his back. Then they tied a scarf around his head so that he couldn't see and led him somewhere where he was made to climb into the rear of some kind of vehicle.

When he opened his eyes later in the day, he couldn't remember how he got to the place he recognized as the diesel shop owned by Stovepipe or why he had even been brought there in the first place.

Was all of this a dream? His life. Was it all a dream? Had he actually even left this place and gotten on the *Storm Roamer*, and met up with Mara—and Joe—and Anna? Taken the seiners to Dutch Harbor? Hired a guy named Hamlet? Found Derrk? Lost Derrk? Had it all been just a dream?

He rubbed his eyes. How he hated headaches and this one was a doozy.

"Gotcha a bed fixed up over in the house," Ted said. "Stovepipe's gonna be away for a while and said you might as well use it. It's better than in here. Only one there'll be you and a couple of bodyguards."

Doug squinted at the man he knew as Stovepipe's lead mechanic.

"It's more 'n comfortable," Ted said. "Just don't get any ideas about leavin'. This whole place is under video surveillance and there are silent alarms pretty much everywhere. Even if you manage to get away, we're gonna find you, and if it comes to that, things'll be a lot tougher on you."

Doug didn't respond.

"Just try to trust Stovepipe. Even though you don't want to."

Chapter Forty-Six

Interesting . . .

Was that Ben talking to Stovepipe over in the corner of the shop? Doug Williams rubbed his eyes and shook off the remnants of last night's deep and refreshing sleep.

No way! He rubbed his eyes again, but by the time his focus cleared, only Stovepipe remained in the shop.

Doug grabbed a cup of coffee from the pot near the exit and walked back to the house. Had things gotten so bad that he was imagining people now? Maybe it was because he had been thinking of Anna and wondering if her mother, Ellie, and her husband, Ben Donaley, knew that she was not in college.

Or maybe it was because in many of the deep troubles that had plagued him in the past, Ben Donaley had always seemed to arrive in the nick of time to help him out. Strange, being that he was the father of Mara's first husband, Brad, and even stranger that he was now married to the widow of his own brother, Dan.

He would never forgive the drug lords who had killed Dan and he knew that Ben Donaley would never forgive them either, but at least Ben and Ellie were happily married now. Even though Ben was almost a full generation older than his new wife, age certainly hadn't slowed him down. He and Ellie had recently had a baby.

Doug finished his coffee and then stepped into the shower. The hot water felt refreshing. Thank god his headache was gone, not that being here now wasn't enough to bring it back at any moment. What was going on anyway? Why had Stovepipe really brought him here and why was he continuing to wear that metal pipe on his leg unless for some reason he needed to maintain his undercover persona? That being said, why was it that he had let a complete stranger like himself in on the ruse—if ruse was the right word for all this?

He had some breakfast and walked back over to the garage. There was no one there but Ted, so he nodded, said nothing, and walked around the yard. He watched a few customers come and go and even lent a hand when Ted asked him to move one of the trucks into the shop.

The temptation to take it and peel on away from there had been great, but for some unknown reason, he had resisted the urge to flee. So far Stovepipe had been straight with him and Ted was himself a fine man. To a guy like Doug Williams, those things mattered.

By midafternoon, Stovepipe had returned, along with another detective, who had set up a secure line to Mara.

"As far as she knows, you're on the *Storm Roamer* right now," Stovepipe said. "You copy that?"

Doug shifted his gaze from the phone to the detective, and then to Stovepipe before nodding his understanding. Then he talked to his wife, even making up something about not being able to leave the boat due to a leak in the hull that required emergency measures, along with his desire that she remain out of sight.

"I can see the *Storm Roamer* from here," she whispered, "and I feel so comforted to know that you're inside."

"You just stay low," Doug answered, "and keep your eyes open at all times. You've got Thor, right?"

"Yes," she answered.

"Then keep Thor and your pistol both near at all times, hear me?"

"Yes."

"I gotta go."

With that he hung up, before the lump that threatened to close off his throat could get any bigger, and before he bared all and told her exactly where he was right now.

"Good work, Williams," Stovepipe said.

"Now remember what I told you. Trust me, whether you feel like it or not."

Doug Williams looked into the eyes of the man who now controlled everything that mattered in his life and nodded. Then he turned and walked back to the house, had a beer, crawled into bed and slept until morning.

Chapter Forty-Seven

Warning

Mara fumbled for the keys to the cabin. Like many rural Alaskans, neither she nor Sal normally locked the door, but lately they had changed their thinking on that front.

Where was that danged key anyway? She was used to having a key-less entry and the whole key thing was frustrating and inconvenient. After not finding it in either pocket of her down jacket, she reached into her jeans, failing to find anything there except for several pieces of note-sized paper that she quickly sifted through and stuffed back inside until she could figure out what they were for. Maybe it was in that tiny pocket inside the pocket that so many jeans had. She checked there. Nothing.

Finally she remembered that she had decided to tuck it into a pocket on the outside of her sleeve and sure enough, when she checked, there it was. What a relief! She walked around the cabin, checking for any signs of disturbance and after finding none, put the key into the lock, turned it, pushed the door open, and went inside.

The cabin smelled closed in, as if no one had been there for a while. Not wanting to leave the door open, she went into both bedrooms and opened the windows to air the place out. Then she found a pile of old bananas and a loaf of stale bread that she threw into the trash.

After several minutes, when the cabin had cooled off and the air smelled fresh and clean, she closed the windows for security and made herself a cup of coffee, while Thor lay down in front of the woodstove for a nap. Although the fire had gone out and nothing but embers and ashes remained inside, the stove still felt warm and Thor had learned to enjoy the comfort of the stove heat years ago.

Mara found some dirty dishes left from when she and Sal had bolted from the cabin, so she filled the sink with soapy water and washed them, enjoying the feel of the hot water on her hands. Then she took a cup of fresh coffee to the table that overlooked the woods, propped her feet up on one of the chairs and rifled through her pockets again in an effort to get rid of all the pieces of paper she had been stuffing into them since the last time she had cleaned it out.

She found a couple of receipts from the grocery store and three sticky notes in the mess. After quickly scanning the receipts, she threw them in the basket, and then began to read the notes. They were written in the deliberate, but somewhat shaky hand that she recognized as Joe Michael's. How they had gotten into her pocket was anybody's guess, but aside from the turned-down corners, they looked to have not been there all that long.

She began to read:

FREE FEATHER
FALL FEATHER
LIFT FEATHER
DOWN

RED DOT
NO DOT
ALWAYS
ROUND

FREE FEATHER
FALL FEATHER
CARRY ME
AWAY

Red dot
Always there
Danger held
At bay
—Joe Michael

It had been a long time since Joe Michael had written one of his ditties. The thought of it made her tremble, not so much from what he had said, but from the understanding that this was a warning from the old man who had sworn to her father that he would protect her for the rest of his life.

She tried to imagine when and how he had put it in her pocket, grasping to understand just where in this recent onslaught of dramatic occurrences he had been prompted to warn her. The ditty hadn't been there when they found the devastation at Joe's home site in Hoonah—of this she was positive.

It hadn't been there when she and Sal had returned to Dutch Harbor either. How then had he made it appear? She took a long sip of coffee. What was the point in trying to understand the whens and whys of the ditty? Experience had taught her that when such a note appeared, danger was near, and so she carefully folded the papers, placed them inside her jacket sleeve next to the key, and gazed quietly at the scene outside her window.

Then she got up, packed a few things into a duffel bag, hooked a leash onto Thor, and walked away from the cabin, telling no one and leaving no notice of when she had been there or if she planned to return.

Chapter Forty-Eight

Faith

As things turned out, it proved to have been a smart move on Mara's part to grab some clothes, because later that day, when she met Sal on the trail on the way back to the cabin, Sal rushed up to her, reached out, turned her around and told her to keep moving.

"They ransacked the cabin," Sal said. "I don't know what they were looking for, but somebody was looking for something—and I found this."

Mara gasped as Sal held up yet another gray bandana with an orange volcano printed on the side.

"I've already talked to Stormy and she wants me to take you personally to the apartment that Justin Smith rented for you."

"But what about the barista who lives there now?" Mara asked.

Sal stopped and looked her daughter straight in the eye.

"The truth is, Mara, that she isn't a barista."

What had happened to the Sal persona? Why was her mother speaking in the real voice of Sylvia LaMonte?

"What is happening?" Mara asked softly, fighting the urge to push Sal/Sylvia aside and run.

"What is happening?!" she screamed.

Sylvia LaMonte drew in a deep breath, followed quickly by two more before answering.

"The barista is a cop, Mara. And her name is Barb."

"How do you know this?" Mara asked.

"I've known it for a while," Sylvia LaMonte answered. "Ever since Jocelyn Sanders told me."

"What is happening?" Mara repeated, "How could this be happening again? How? And why does it seem that everyone is a cop? Are you a cop, too? Are you, Sylvia?"

Sylvia LaMonte watched as her only child stood at the verge of hysteria. She had often read that motherhood was hard, but as she was now learning, it was much harder and in a much different way than she had ever imagined.

She reached for Mara's hand, only to feel her daughter draw back and pull it away, and then she looked into Mara's eyes, only to see them look away.

Neither Sylvia LaMonte nor her persona as Sal Kindle had ever been the type to display emotion, but this time, Mara's mother fought back tears at the pain she saw on her daughter's face.

This is not about you, she reminded herself.

Turning back to Mara, she said, "The barista's name is Barb and Jocelyn Sanders wants me to take you to her, then she wants me to leave Dutch Harbor. She has assured me that you will be safe—Thor, too."

Mara didn't answer. Instead she just stood there stroking Thor's head.

"I'm going to take you to Barb tonight, then I'm going to take the red eye out of here to Juneau, after which the FBI will fly me to Sitka to be with Joey."

Sal waited a few minutes and when Mara still didn't speak she said, "Leaving you like this is the hardest thing I've ever done. I know I did it once and after I found you, I swore that I would never do it again, but I know Stormy and if Stormy says I need to go, then I need to go. And if Stormy says you'll be safe, then you'll be safe, so, as she said in the cabin the other day, the word to remember is *faith*.

"Faith, Mara—faith in Jocelyn Sanders, faith in yourself, and last of all, faith in me."

With those words, Sylvia LaMonte walked her only daughter up to the door of the apartment where she had once lived as Alisa Allison, rang the doorbell, and silently handed her daughter over to the cop named Barb.

"I'm taking Thor with me," she said as she left. "He'll be safe that way. And by the way, no, I'm not a cop."

Chapter Forty-Nine

Early Strategy

"This is going to get pretty nasty pretty quickly," Hamlet told Anna, who had been returned to the *Storm Roamer* once Doug had been moved to the care of Stovepipe.

Anna nodded. She understood why Doug couldn't know where she was, but that understanding did not make it any easier for her to not feel for the suffering and worry that he must be going through.

"What we need to do over the next couple of days is to get very familiar—and I'm talking *very* familiar with every inch of this seiner."

Anna nodded again.

"There can't be one function, one nook or cranny, or one situation that we could find ourselves in that we would not be able to respond to without hesitation."

"Okay," Anna replied.

She had been assigned to Hamlet as his rookie for six months now and the two of them had developed a mutual respect. She had learned early on that he was as experienced as he was gruff and he had learned that she was as tough as she was soft.

"Now that Doug's been moved to Kenai, and Mara is safe with Barb, we can move forward without fear of endangering either of them."

"What about Sal?" Anna asked. "And Joe Michael?"

"They'll be together again by tonight and under the direct supervision of his friend John's son, who has been one of our agents for years."

"Wow! Even I didn't know that," Anna replied.

"Few people do," Hamlet answered, "but be assured that it's no mistake that he found a way to lure Joe Michael back to Sitka and made sure by damaging his work there that Joe had good reason to stay."

"I'm thinking that Joe Michael will feel that the damage had deeper meaning than that once he finds out," Anna said.

"There's no doubt, then, that it was the perfect way to distract him," Hamlet said. "And who's to say there isn't more to it anyway. I mean, I belie—never mind." Hamlet abruptly changed the subject.

Anna didn't press him. As a lifelong Alaskan, she knew full well that the changes to Joe Michael's work had been more than symbolic—if that was the right word. Secret FBI agent or not, John's son and any alterations he had made to the totem had meant something, or at the minimum, had been so skillfully considered that no one outside of law enforcement would ever have reason to doubt the deeper significance of what had been done.

"I think that when this is over you should go there, "Anna said.

"Yeah, maybe . . ."

"I think you should do it," she repeated, looking right into his eyes. "You know, for yourself."

"I will, then," he answered. "I will."

Anna grabbed a flashlight and began exploring every nook and cranny in the galley. She then moved into the sleeping quarters and did the same before crawling down into the hold to see exactly what was down there, almost gagging on the overpowering stench of fish slime.

"One thing we need to do is to hose that hold down again," she said, coughing as she climbed back out. "But I did find a trap door down there that leads into some kind of compartment."

"Seriously?" Hamlet answered.

"Check it out," she said.

She waited for Hamlet to crawl down into the hold and listened to a series of knocks and bangs interspersed with a few choice words as he worked the trap door loose.

When he climbed back out a short while later, the look on his face said almost as much as the words he spoke.

"There's a space down there that's about three feet wide and maybe ten feet long. I can't even imagine why it's there, maybe some kind of hull protection thing—don't know. The fact of it is, though, it was dry—totally dry—and if you peeled back a section of rubber-rimmed gasket, you can see through the slats of the galley floor."

"Wow!" Anna said. "Some kind of ventilated storage area . . ."

"Exactly!" Hamlet said. "Didn't you tell me that your Uncle Doug said that the *Storm Roamer* and the *Driftfeather* were identical seiners?"

"Supposedly," she answered.

"Then we need to get onto the *Driftfeather* and verify that," Hamlet said.

"I could talk to Derrk," Anna said. "He's worked with Uncle Doug for ages."

"That's exactly the point, Anna," he said, looking at her sideways.

Anna blushed.

"You don't mean—you can't be saying—"

"Keep this between me and you, Anna. If you value your life and the life of everyone involved in this, keep this quiet—and that means you don't tell anyone, not Jocelyn Sanders, not Larry Kenton, definitely not your Uncle or Aunt—no one. Roger that?"

"Roger," she said meekly.

"Look," Hamlet said, "We were all rookies once. You found that hold and that's some good detective work, Agent Williams. As for the rest of it—well that's why they call it teamwork."

Hamlet didn't see her momentary smile. If he had, the vulnerability he had been feeling as of late might have overrun the detached and rigid demeanor he had spent the majority of his career perfecting, right after his daughter had been murdered by an escaped con back in his hometown of Syracuse, New York—a daughter who would have been Anna's age about now.

Chapter Fifty

Captivity

M ara accepted Barb's offer of a glass of water as well as the invitation to join her for stir-fry for dinner. Although the two women engaged in polite and superficial chitchat, their conversation did nothing to answer Mara's questions about why she had been brought here.

"I know what you're thinking," Barb said. "And I wish I could tell you what you want to know, but I can't."

Mara played with her food, pushing it around the plate with her fork.

"You need to trust me," Barb said. "I know that sounds weird."

Mara got up and took her plate to the sink and washed it.

"I know none of this makes sense, okay. I'm guessing that you're also worried about your husband, your mother, and your niece, as well as the old man they call Joe Michael. They're safe. Know that, okay? I guarantee you that they are all safe, and they know you are, too."

Mara sat on the sofa and stared out over the water. What was the point in even asking any questions? Things around her were happening outside of her control, just as they had been for some time now. She had always been okay, even in situations worse than this one.

She reached for the feather, forgetting it was gone. Instead, she found the ditty written by Joe. She knew it was a warning, but about what?

Knowing him, it definitely warned of danger. She reminded herself to read it again later, when she was alone. She thought about Doug. Was he thinking about her? At least they had had that night together a few days ago. It felt like longer. Everything did as each day passed by with excruciating slowness, despite incredible activity.

She closed her eyes. When she opened them again it was dark, and she was stretched out on Barb's sofa, not sure where the blanket that covered her had come from. When she got up to use the restroom, she heard Barb snoring softly in one of the bedrooms. Only then did she see the other guard in the room, an older man with a potbelly and two sidearms—one on each hip.

"Ma'am," he nodded.

She continued to the restroom, nodding when she came back out, and then silently crawled under the blanket again. Feigning sleep, she tried to remember the words to Joe Michael's ditty that she had just read in the bathroom. She had intentionally tried to memorize it, but the words weren't coming to her as fast as she wanted them to. And then, there they were:

FREE FEATHER
FALL FEATHER
LIFT FEATHER
DOWN

RED DOT
NO DOT
ALWAYS
ROUND

FREE FEATHER
FALL FEATHER
CARRY ME
AWAY

RED DOT
ALWAYS THERE
DANGER HELD
AT BAY

It was the last stanza that stuck with her—the part about the red dot always being there and holding danger at bay.

Did that mean that she had to physically have the feather and the red dot for it to work or did it mean that once she had seen the red dot, and held it and touched it that it would always be with her?

She told herself to stop overthinking it, but her mind wouldn't listen. Finally, at long last, she fell asleep again.

Chapter Fifty-One

Planning the Top-Secret Plan

Hamlet paced the galley long after Anna had retired for the night. He had debated whether or not to tell her about the bag of new bandanas he had found in the space off the hold. Sure, she was his rookie, but this case was bigger than anything he had ever been involved in before.

The case was so big and so dangerous, in fact, that law enforcement had taken the extraordinary step of practically imprisoning Doug and Mara Williams, who they believed to be in imminent danger from the known entity whose identity they were keeping as closely a guarded secret as any that had gone before.

Risky as it was, he summoned his supervisor, texting him in code and asking him to meet at the end of the dock. There they would be out of view of the seiner, but still in the path of anyone who might approach the *Storm Roamer* from the street.

Once Ben Donaley arrived, Hamlet handed him the bag of bandanas and explained where he had found them. He went on to explain that he suspected a similar hidden compartment would be found in the *Storm Roamer's* sister ship, the *Driftfeather,* but that his gut told him not to trust such a search to Derrl or Joey Stanley, J.D. Smith, or Cory, no matter how trustworthy they were or who they were working for.

"There's no one I trust more than you, Del," Ben Donaley said, referring to Hamlet by his given name. "That's why you were the only person I would trust to watch out for my step-daughter, Anna, and for Doug and Mara, who are like a son and daughter to me."

Delbert Green brushed off the compliment, all the while knowing that Ben Donaley had meant every bit of what he said about trusting the man he had worked side by side with for over thirty years. What he hadn't figured out just yet was why it was that he was choosing not to trust Doug William's longtime trusted employee, or the other three men whose identities, although known to him, could not even be revealed in his conscious mind just yet.

"I'm just sayin' that we need to hatch us a plan," Hamlet said. "A plan that everyone will buy into—and that means without arousing suspicion on any level."

"Lay it on me," Ben Donaley said, knowing without being told that Hamlet had already come up with something.

Hamlet outlined every detail of his idea for conducting a secret inspection of the *Driftfeather*, including who would be where when the inspection came down. Then he told Ben Donaley that if his suspicions about the *Drifteather* were confirmed, the operation dubbed *Ultimate Danger* would begin to unfold.

"First I gotta be a hundred percent sure I'm right," Hamlet said, "and right now I'm only 99.9 percent sure, know what I mean, man?"

"Okay, Del," Ben Donaley said. "We'll let this play out however you decide."

"Well, chief, the stakes have never been higher and if I'm wrong—if I don't call this just right, if I've missed a signal, or misread what I think is coming down—then we're gonna have a whole lot more to worry about than what I'm thinkin' I'm about to expose."

Ben Donaley nodded.

"Don't worry, chief, " Hamlet said, "Anna can take care of herself. Trust that."

Ben Donaley scowled, not sure if he was doing so because deep down inside maybe he disagreed, or because he knew he would never be able to face his wife again if anything happened to her daughter.

"Chief," Hamlet called as Ben Donaley walked away, "why don't you practice a little of what you preach to me all the time and keep the faith. Like you're always saying, goodness will prevail."

"Yeah, I know Del, but it's all that happens before goodness seeps into these situations that has me worried."

Chapter Fifty-Two

Unretired—for Now

Interim Director for Special Operations of the FBI Ben Donaley walked up to the street and directed the seven special agents who had been assigned to guard Anna Williams and the *Storm Roamer* to their respective posts. Even though assigning this number of agents could be viewed as overkill, years of experience in dealing with this level of criminal activity had taught him that it wasn't.

At first he had been reluctant to come out of retirement—that is, until he had learned exactly what the assignment involved. Once he did, he had quickly stepped up into the lead role, knowing full well that he had more vested interest in this particular lawless alliance than anyone else on the force; not needing to remind himself that he had long ago vowed that he would work until his last breath on earth to stop the evil that had for so long been wrought by one of the most aggressive, subversive, and pervasive criminal forces on earth.

As much as he remained unsurprised by this recent turn of events, Ben had to admit that he had never wanted to believe that it would come to this. And why Doug and Mara? Silly rhetorical question. He knew why. Doug was Dan's younger brother and Dan had become the cause célèbre of a twisted and subversive revenge plot that had actually targeted him via his own son, Brad.

With both Brad and Dan now dead, with him now married to Dan's widow, Ellie (whose daughter was rookie agent Anna Williams), and with Brad's widow, Mara, now married to Dan's brother, Doug, the whole family had been targeted by both the original players and the subsequent followers of the South American drug cartels, whose thinking—according to testimony from one of their own, Carlos Antoya—had been that all family members would be eliminated slowly and methodically before Ben Donaley himself would become the hit. Sadly, that list had also included Joe Michael and his wife, Sal, both of whom were now being secretly guarded in Sitka.

They had done this in a variety of ways, while maintaining their illegal drug-running operations, often letting innocent people take the hit for their activities, even if it meant crimes such as murder, theft, smuggling, and extortion—including arranging the accident of family members, like the wife of Agent Delbert Green, aka Hamlet.

Ben Donaley felt a slight flutter in his chest. If Ellie knew what he was up to, she would be upset, so he hadn't told her, instead sending her to New York with her sister and the new baby, telling her to take a nice long month's vacation while he took care of some other things that could not wait.

Ellie had reluctantly gone back, knowing that arguing with Ben would be futile. Besides, Sarah would be so happy to see her old friends there and the two sisters would enjoy all that shopping and trips to see Broadway plays that Ben always found so boring, even if it meant taking the baby along with them.

Ben sat on a log railing to rest. One of his men came up to clarify some point and the two men talked briefly before getting up and moving their separate ways. He had done all he could to protect Anna from any type of assault from above or below the water, and all without her even having a clue that he was even in Dutch Harbor.

Ben thought of fellow agents Larry Allen Kenton and Jocelyn Sanders as he walked. Boy did they all go way back! He smiled at the thought, before furrowing his brow and feeling another flip-flop in his chest.

For his own health and safety, he needed to stop thinking for a while. Wasn't that why he had brought Hamlet onto the case? He stopped for a beer on his way to the airport, then climbed aboard the chartered flight to Kodiak and slept through the five-and-a-half-hour flight. Once the plane had landed, he grabbed a bite to eat at an all-night café, then headed to his hotel room for the night, checking in using an alternate ID as a fish broker from Seattle.

He had already called Ellie on a secure line from Anchorage, with caller ID construed to look like he was calling from home. The laughter in her voice made him smile almost as much as did knowing that she and the baby were safe from harm.

Chapter Fifty-Three

Solitude

While Anna slept through the night, Hamlet walked the streets of Dutch Harbor. For one thing, he liked the cover of darkness, although this time of year, there wasn't all that much of that. He also liked the solitude, because it gave him time to think.

Ben Donaley had been smart to leave the island. He wouldn't have wanted anything to happen to the man he had worked with for over thirty years, and this time, he had a strong gut feeling that this whole situation was going to turn out to be bigger than any of them had feared. Even he was worried and not much worried him at this point in a career that had pretty much seen it all.

He walked up past the apartment where Mara was being protected. He would have felt better if they had gotten her out of Dutch, but that hadn't panned out. Barb would keep an eye on her, though.

He walked up the hill past the cabin owned by Sal's friend. It looked empty. He'd heard it had been ransacked. Seeing it reminded him of Sitka and the knowledge that Sal and Joe were safe. Good. Then he stopped and sat on a rock near the trail and ate an apple. Probably not all that smart of an idea in the wilds, but he was hungry. A snap behind him made him jump up and start walking again. He caught a glimpse of a fox running near where he had been sitting.

It wasn't like him to be jumpy and he didn't like feeling vulnerable like that.

He made his way back into the town center and stopped at the ship supply store that also carried groceries, hardware, and all manner of products. There he stocked up on food and a few cleaning supplies, before reaching for a six-pack of beer to take back to the seiner, just in case he needed to calm his nerves.

For some reason he thought about Della. He'd only met her twice, but each time he had been left with an uneasy feeling. Was it because she was Native? He laughed out loud. Being a black man had taught him about prejudice for sure, so he wiped the thought from his mind.

By the time he got back to the *Storm Roamer* it was midnight and he was surprised to find Anna in the galley.

"Needed a midnight snack, I guess," she told him.

He put the groceries away and snapped the tab on a beer.

"Why'd they assign me to you?" she asked, seemingly out of nowhere.

"Guess they wanted to toughen you up," he laughed.

"I'm tougher than you think," she answered.

"That's what they all say," Hamlet said.

"You'll see," she told him.

Hamlet set his beer down and looked squarely at the youngest FBI rookie he had ever met.

"Look, Anna," he began. "I don't want to soft-soap this."

"What?"

"I want to be square with you."

"I wouldn't have it any other way," she answered.

"The mission that you and I have been assigned to is probably the most dangerous mission of my career—and I've seen a lot in thirty years," he laughed.

"Okay," she said.

"I know you say you're tough, and I believe you, don't get me wrong, but tough might not be enough when this thing comes down, so you're going to need to learn to keep your head on straight, keep your wits about you, stay calm, and stay low if need be."

"Okay."

"And whatever happens, I want you to know that as long as I'm alive, I'll come find you."

"Okay," she said again.

Why was he telling her this? Didn't it go without saying? She squirmed a little in her seat.

"You go get yourself some good sleep," Hamlet said. "Nothing's coming down tonight. And as for me, I'm gonna do likewise. Goodnight."

With that, Hamlet got up and went to his bunk, leaving Anna sitting in the galley feeling just a tad more anxious than she had told herself she would.

Chapter Fifty-Four

Old Alliances

Ted hadn't seen the fist coming that knocked him into the stratosphere, although he did find it wryly amusing that Doug Williams had taken the time to pin a note to his shirt.

SORRY, MAN ... NOTHING PERSONAL ... I GOT THINGS TO TAKE CARE OF ...

"How the ..." Stovepipe said as he helped Ted up off the floor. "You okay?"

"Never saw it comin'," Ted mumbled. "Dang!"

"Never underestimate a man with determination," Stovepipe said. "Even if he doesn't mind taking the last chance he might have to save his sorry life."

~~~

Doug Williams had hitched a ride to Anchorage before the APB even went out. By the time his picture had been plastered all over Facebook, he had shaved his head and begun the growth of a beard that by all appearances was destined to come in red. He had even taken to wearing a bandana and had gotten one ear pierced, which Mara was definitely going to have issues with—maybe.

He had owned a couple of Harleys, so there was little adjustment there. As far as he knew, no one in his current life knew anything about his friend, Anvil, who was more than willing to let Doug run with him and his buddies in a biker group that was more talk than outlaw—although make no mistake, they could rise to the occasion when necessary.

The fact of the matter was that Anvil and Doug had fished together for several years before going their separate ways when Anvil hurt his back and was off work for a year during which his wife left him for another man.

"You oughtta come fish on my seiner, dude," said Doug, who was now going by the name of Booger. "This biker life's gotta be getting old."

But Anvil just straddled his Harley, and gunned the engine a couple of times for effect, before waving at Doug to follow him. He hadn't even asked that many questions about what Doug was doing on the run. He didn't need to. The two trusted each other and always had, going back to a time when Doug had pushed Anvil out of the way of a falling fish brailer.

Whatever was going on, Doug was welcome to ride with the boys, according to Anvil, until things settled down—no questions asked, and so Doug had bought one of Anvil's old bikes and joined the Wolverines, even wearing their colors without the usual crime spree ritual that awarded one such a privilege.

"I don't know what you're running from, my friend," Anvil said. "But I know it's gotta be bad for you to hook up with my gang."

After which Doug had filled his friend in on the whole saga, starting back with the death of his brother, Dan, the resurgence of Mara's first husband, their own marriage and divorce, and the entire litany of crises he had endured over the past few years, including this current one.

"Well, if anyone's running drugs or worse here in the Valley—or anywhere in South Central I'm gonna know about it. I'll put some feelers out there to see what I can find out. I'll let you know if your name comes up."

"Fair enough," Doug said. "I appreciate you and the guys taking me in for a while."

"No problem, friend," Anvil answered. "I know you ain't gonna mess with us, and besides, I owe you—like I said before."

For the next few weeks, Doug ran with Anvil and the Wolverines, doing nothing more than becoming one with them. During that time, he made no effort to contact Mara, Joe, or Sal, or anyone from either the *Driftfeather* of the *Storm Roamer*. As for the cops, although they meant well, they didn't really know what they were up against like he did and this time the stakes were too high for him to sit back and watch them get overrun with the antics of the South American cartel.

He had been sure it was them from the get-go. No matter what the cops thought. The only lingering question in his mind was, why him and Mara, and why Joe and Sal?

Chapter Fifty-Five

Lashing Out

Mara was relieved when she finally heard from Doug, who assured her that he was safe and bored and minding his P's and Q's. She didn't buy the story any more than he bought hers about being content to live inside Barb's apartment.

"Look, I don't know who's monitoring our calls, okay," he said.

Mara knew what he was trying to say.

"I've got a bag packed at all times."

"Love you," he said.

"Love you, too," she answered.

Mara walked over to the sofa and sat sideways, looking out the window.

"You two sure are a lovey-dovey pair," Barb said.

When Mara didn't respond, Barb continued, "I hope you two aren't up to something like so many we try to protect that think they can handle things better on their own."

"Like, where am I supposed to go?" Mara asked.

Barb raised one eyebrow. Who could blame her, actually? She'd probably be just as hostile. Worse!

"Look, Mara, I think we got off on the wrong foot. How about if I start by apologizing for my sometimes abrupt demeanor and my tendency toward sarcasm?"

"Yeah, okay," Mara answered. "I feel the love, okay?"

"Well, it's gonna take more than just me to make this work, babykins," Barb retorted.

"Pardon me, officer, but I think I'll turn in early tonight," Mara said, getting up and heading to the bedroom.

"Look, for what it's worth, I care," Barb said.

'Yup, I know," Mara said without turning back.

Barb was okay, and she had defended her when everyone was talking after Justin Smith got shot. Besides, it wasn't Barb's fault that she was even in this mess.

If she didn't feel bad already, she was really starting to now. She missed Doug. She was worried about Sal and Joe. She wondered where Della was and what had happened to the feather, and she wondered why Joe had written her that latest poem.

She got into bed and read it and then she read it again.

Free feather
fall feather
Lift feather
down

Red dot
No dot
Always
Round

Free feather
Fall feather
Carry me
Away

Red dot
Always there
Danger held
At bay

She wasn't sure how many times she said it in her head before sleep overcame her, but its words gave her comfort, and hope—as if the feather itself were still in her pocket.

When she awoke and met Barb for coffee in the kitchen, she said, "I'm sorry, Barb, for the way I acted. I really mean it. I'm sorry. You didn't deserve it."

"It's alright," Barb answered. "I understand. Really. I get it. I'd be the same way."

"I need to color my hair," Mara said. "Got a few grays coming in. Want to help me?"

"Only if you want to be totally freaky wild and do something fun," Barb answered. "Like put in some teal highlights or play around with lowlights and highlights . . ."

"Works for me as long as you don't pull out the scissors," Mara laughed, "And only if turnabout's fair play."

The two women spent the afternoon doing those things that women so enjoy: hair, nails, pedicures, before dining on Chinese food that Barb had brought in.

"That was great!" Mara told the woman who had been assigned to protect her. "Really, it was a lot of fun. I like you, Barb, and I truly am grateful that you're looking out for me."

"Thanks, Mara," Barb answered. "I'm giving it all I've got."

Chapter Fifty-Six

Gone

M ara stopped when she heard voices as she stepped out of the bathroom. Barb hadn't said anything about company. She waited in the hallway as the discussion continued, becoming uneasy as it began heating up.

She peeked around the corner to see Captain Jocelyn Sanders in an intense discussion with Barb, one in which neither she nor Barb looked any too happy.

"It's not the first time I've cautioned you about getting too close to the people you're guarding, Barb."

"I'm well aware of my professional boundaries, captain."

"I'm afraid I would have to disagree with that assessment, Barb."

"Just because someone is in my care doesn't mean that—"

"This case is too important for me to accept this act of insubordination, Barb. It's unacceptable and I can't tolerate it. I'll have another deputy here within the hour, after which I am pulling you off the case."

Mara had heard all she needed to hear. For reasons that she could totally not understand, Jocelyn Sanders was acting like she was some kind of fugitive from justice. Despite the fact that Sal had told her to trust the head of the investigation team, Mara took less than five minutes to find her bag, throw in her blow dryer, pry open the bathroom window, which had been only loosely nailed shut, and climb outside to freedom with Joe Michael's words ringing in her head.

FREE FEATHER
FALL FEATHER
LIFT FEATHER
DOWN

RED DOT
NO DOT
ALWAYS
ROUND

FREE FEATHER
FALL FEATHER
CARRY ME
AWAY

RED DOT
ALWAYS THERE
DANGER HELD
AT BAY

Mara Williams would take her chances with the bears and the wolves and the roving drunks of Dutch Harbor. She would take her chances with the weather and the elements and the dangers that darkness brings, but she would not remain a sitting duck under the care of feuding and uncoordinated FBI agents, that was for sure, and she would not sit back and pass control of her own destiny to strangers.

And so, under the cover of darkness, she made her way through town and back to the cabin where she and Sal had once found safety. Police tape still surrounded it, but she found the door unlocked and went inside. She would sleep a couple of hours and then move to a more secure location. Where that was, how she would get there undetected, and what she would do about the fact that police would now be actively looking for her was unclear, but in no way, shape, or form was she staying with Barb, Jocelyn Sanders, or any of the rest of law enforcement. She would rather take her chances alone and let destiny take her where it would.

She chanted the words of Joe Michael as she drifted into a sound sleep:

FREE FEATHER

FALL FEATHER

LIFT FEATHER

DOWN

RED DOT

NO DOT

ALWAYS . . .

Chapter Fifty-Seven

Unbelievable

For the next three days, Mara wandered the streets of Dutch Harbor, Alaska, somehow managing to escape detection. Maybe no one was looking for her. She laughed at the thought. You don't just walk away from the cops in this world. As much as she knew that, though, she had still done it. What had happened to the sweet and naïve person she used to be? Was she now a criminal? Was that how it happened— one day you are a normal person and the next day you are a fugitive from the law, all because somebody decided to mess with your life?

It was only after a close call with the cops at the public showers that she decided to make her move. She had to get to Doug. He would know what to do. Calling him was too risky, so she waited until dark and sneaked down the docks to the *Storm Roamer*, nearly falling into the harbor when a sea lion rose out of the water and threatened to jump up to do god knew what.

Things seemed pretty quiet around the seiner as she lifted her bag over the side and reached as far as she could so it wouldn't make much noise when it dropped. She waited a full five minutes before climbing over herself. So far, so good. She could see someone sitting at the table in the galley. It was a woman, who was cleaning a pistol. Strange. Doug hadn't said anything about hiring a woman deckhand. Not that she was worried. She trusted him fully.

She picked up her bag and made a little noise, prompting the woman in the galley to spin around and Mara to jump back in case the woman had another gun. Mara reached for her own piece, and with her hand firmly on it in its holster, she slowly walked forward until suddenly stopping in her tracks.

"Aunt Mara?" Anna said.

"Anna? Where's Doug?"

Anna walked to Mara and embraced her.

"Come with me and stay as quiet as you can. No one can know you're here."

What was happening? Why was Anna here and where was Doug?

"I need to talk to you, Aunt Mara, but not right now. No one can know you're here. I can't believe that you got this far without being detected."

Mara looked around and saw no sign of her husband.

"Where's Doug?" she whispered.

"He's safe," Anna answered. "But he's not here. Look, Hamlet is going to be going into town as soon as he gets up. Until then, I'm going to put you in the hold until I figure out what to do. I know it's rank down there, but there's a compartment down there with an air hole and you'll be able to see a little into the galley here and you'll understand, okay."

Who was Hamlet and why was Anna being so skittish?

"Just do what I said, Aunt Mara. Please. I'll explain as soon as Hamlet leaves."

Something told Mara to listen to her niece and so she went down into the hold and opened the door to the secret compartment. Although she didn't go all the way inside just yet, she was close enough to hear Hamlet when he woke up.

"Did I hear something, Anna? That beer made me sleep harder than I figured."

"One of the undercover agents came aboard to make rounds," she lied. "I asked him to because I didn't want to bother you while you were sleeping. I knew how tired you were."

Hamlet scowled, then rubbed his eyes.

"Got any coffee, rookie?"

Anna brought him a steaming cup of strong coffee.

"It's not going to happen again," Hamlet said.

"What do you mean?"

"The beer. I won't do that again. I need to keep my wits about me."

"I was fine. I handled it," Anna answered.

Hamlet scowled again.

"You were lucky it wasn't something worse," he replied. "Now keep things buttoned up here till I get back."

"Yes, sir," Anna said. "I copy that."

Chapter Fifty-Eight

Shock and Awe

Anna followed Hamlet out of the galley and followed him up the dock as he left.

"What're you doing?" he asked her.

"Look, I need to talk to you."

"We'll talk later, when I get back."

"I need to talk to you now."

"Then why didn't you talk over coffee?"

Anna fumbled for words. Hamlet was her superior and he could be tough and intimidating. He also had a reputation for having a very low tolerance for insubordination.

"I don't know how to tell you this," she began.

"Okay, Anna," Hamlet said, trying hard to keep his irritation from showing.

"That was no agent coming to check on me that you heard last night."

"What!" he said, spinning around.

"It was . . ." Anna gulped and then measured her words. "It was Mara Williams, Doug Williams's wife and my aunt."

"What the …!" Hamlet said.

"I didn't know what to do or what to tell her. She's down in the hold right now. All I told her was that Doug was safe and that I would talk to her after you left. She saw me cleaning my pistol . . . that's all she knows."

"Great!" Hamlet said with the sardonic inflection that meant *not*.

"I didn't tell Barb, I didn't call Jocelyn, I told no one," Anna said. "I didn't even tell Mara that I was with the FBI."

Hamlet lit a cigarette, pacing and inhaling deep puffs of smoke.

"Okay, first off, she's safe and that's priority one," he said. "And secondly, until we ask her we can't know, but from everything I know about your aunt, she wouldn't have pulled this without a reason."

"That's right," Anna said. "I mean, she can be headstrong, but she's no fugitive or anything."

Hamlet nodded and started walking back to the *Storm Roamer*.

"Do you want me to call Barb, or Captain Sanders?" Anna asked.

"No," Hamlet answered. "Until we know more, we're gonna keep this between me and you, but first, we're gonna have to talk to Mara and find out what made her do this and come clean with who we are and what's going on here."

"You mean, even the part about me?" Anna asked.

"Especially the part about you," he answered. "But before we talk to her, we're going to need to lose some of the security we've got going on around here. Give me a minute here, okay?"

By the time Hamlet returned, no fewer than five secret agents moved past them toward the harbor.

Minutes later, both Anna and Hamlet climbed back aboard the *Storm Roamer* and proceeded to let a pale-looking Mara out of the hold.

"I couldn't have stood the smell much longer," she gasped.

"Anna, get hold of the harbormaster and tell him we need a flush and clean operation sent down here ASAP. He'll know someone."

Then Hamlet turned to Mara and introduced himself as Delbert Green of the FBI.

"And though I know that you know Anna here as your niece, she is also special agent Anna Williams, rookie FBI agent on special assignment to me."

Although it would have seemed impossible for Mara to look any paler, suddenly she did. Then she sat down, put her arms on the table, laid her head on top of them, and closed her eyes.

"Are you okay, Mrs. Williams?" Hamlet asked.

Finally, she nodded before reaching out for both Hamlet and Anna with her two hands.

"I'm just so tired . . . all the running . . . it never stops . . ."

"With all due respect, Mrs. Williams," Hamlet said, "That's as sad a story as maybe the hundred and fifty thousand others I've heard in my life—"

"Don't talk to her that way," Anna said, jumping up.

Hamlet ignored the outburst and continued.

"The point is, that you've got the rest of your life to rest up, Mrs. Williams, but that's only if we succeed in stopping the South American cartel forever. Your other option is—well, I don't think you even want to go there."

"I understand," Mara said, regaining her composure.

"What's happening right now is the lining up of the stars, if you will. Look, I haven't even told Anna this yet, but Carlos Antoya broke out of prison two weeks ago and we think he's in Alaska. That's why we had to get Joe Michael out of here. Not only do we think he's in Alaska, but we think he's right here in Dutch Harbor."

Anna and Mara exchanged glances. They had had plenty of opportunity to see Carlos Antoya at work.

"What about Doug?" Mara asked.

"Doug's with Stovepipe—or at least he was."

"What—"

"You two must be pretty compatible, because he broke free of his security detail about three days ago and as far as we know, he's still somewhere up in the Palmer area."

Mara gasped.

"If he's got a brain in his head, he'll get out of the Valley—and Dutch Harbor," Hamlet said. "Until we know for sure, though, we're aggressively looking for him—not because he broke free, but for his own safety, much like the situation with you, Mrs. Williams."

Chapter Fifty-Nine

It's Starting

After much discussion and some lunch, it was decided that Mara would be hidden in the hold, since moving her would leave her without any protection.

"It won't be for long," Hamlet said, "and only during the day when you can be spotted. I think we can manage for you to stay up here much of the day anyway, by just blocking off one of the bunks with a blanket. It shouldn't attract too much attention since we're already operating with a man and a woman aboard and have done some of this stuff already."

Mara reluctantly agreed. What choice did she have? If, as Hamlet had told her, Carlos Antoya was in the area, things would be coming to a head very soon.

"I'm going to have to leave for a couple of hours to get things moving with inspecting the *Driftfeather*," Hamlet said. "I'll be more than amazed if it doesn't have a secret compartment like the one on this seiner—and one that I suspect was and is being used to smuggle in both members of the cartel and contraband."

"Will our security be brought back?" Anna asked.

"I'll bring them with me, but you two will need to stay low for a couple of hours."

Hamlet climbed over the rail of the *Storm Roamer* before turning back to face Mara.

"You've got a pistol. Keep it handy. You, too, Anna."

"And if you hear from anyone on the *Driftfeather,* tell them something—anything. Tell them I'm in the can if you have to, but don't tell them that you're here alone or mention anything about either Doug or Mara."

With those words, Hamlet left as the two women made their way back to the galley, where they pulled the homemade curtains that Anna had made for privacy around the windows.

Afraid to talk for fear of their voices being heard, they exchanged notes, not even taking advantage of the writing program on their phones in case someone had hacked their accounts. When they were done, they burned the notes on the gas stove in the galley and dumped the ashes into the harbor.

Every few minutes, Anna got up and started singing, pretending that she was cleaning the galley or that she was talking to Hamlet. She covered for the fact that he never answered, by making statements about how she hoped he would enjoy his nap and hoped he felt better soon. If anyone had been listening, she hoped she had been believable.

Meanwhile, Mara watched all of this with amazement, noting how grown-up Anna seemed. Although the knowledge that her niece was now with the FBI had come as a shock, in thinking about it since she had come to realize that it made perfect sense that Anna would have chosen this career path. After all, she had long ago formed many very positive alliances with persons in the law enforcement field, including her own stepfather, Ben Donaley, and in her young life, she had witnessed enough criminal activity to fill the lives of three normal people, including the murder of her father, Dan.

Strange, how life had turned out. In many ways she wished that Anna had chosen a less dangerous field, but on the other hand she could totally relate to her niece's wanting to have some sense of control over the evil that had so powerfully affected her life.

"So Doug's known for a while now?" she whispered to Anna.

"Yes," Anna answered.

Then she wrote:

IT WAS KILLING HIM NOT TO TELL YOU. HE TOLD ME MORE THAN ONCE THAT HE HATED TO KEEP SECRETS FROM YOU. WE MADE HIM PROMISE

TO NOT TELL YOU. HE SAID IT WAS ONE OF THE HARDEST DECISIONS HE'S EVER HAD TO MAKE.

Mara smiled, having no doubts that what Anna had written was true. She gave her niece two thumbs up to signal her understanding.

How she wished that she could call her husband and find out where he was and what he was doing. Was he safe? Anna had told her that they had been unable to get word to Doug, and that no one even knew where he was. The thought of that didn't worry her. If he had gotten away on his own, then she knew he was safe. The remaining uncertainty was in not knowing when they would find each other again. It would happen, of this there was no doubt, but from her perspective, it couldn't happen soon enough.

Chapter Sixty

Holy -----!

How Doug had managed to get Anvil to come with him to Unalaska was anybody's guess, but the two had loaded their bikes onto the ferry and taken the lengthy trip to Dutch Harbor and driven across the bridge to Unalaska.

Since it was fishing season, there were enough strangers in town to make the two of them look no weirder than anyone else. Doug had asked Anvil to call him Booger—a name that he had once been called while playing high school football. The two had coordinated their stories. They were there looking for a couple of friends who had been out fishing all month and were coming in soon.

"Stritch owes me money and I know he'll be gettin' paid real soon. Across his palm to my hand is how I look at it," Anvil said to Doug outside the processing plant gate, within earshot of the security guard on duty.

"Mind if we wait?" he said to the guard.

"We don't want no trouble," the guard had warned. "So if you got issues, take 'em somewhere besides here."

The fact that there was no one named Stritch would remain the secret of both Doug and Anvil, but as far as anyone else knew, there were two mean-looking bikers in town waiting for what might be the hypothetical Stritch's last chance to collect one of the huge paychecks known to have brought many a stranger up to fish the dangerous waters of Alaska.

As the two stood by the dock watching crews unload the boats, they leaned back against some rocks just outside the seafood plant property to enjoy the sun, all under the watchful eye of security.

"You oughta come and fish with me when all this is over," Doug told Anvil. "Good pay. Good life. Tough hours though."

"Yeah . . . maybe," Anvil answered.

"You can't be digging this kind of life that much, can you, man?" Doug asked. "Always on edge and lookin' over your shoulder, walkin' around with that big chip on it."

"Like you got room to talk," Anvil shot back.

"Look, I told you my story. Don't mix apples and oranges here," Doug said sharply. "What the ..., Jeff. I know you're better than this."

"Yeah, well up yours, Williams," Anvil answered. "And I cleaned that up just on account of us bein' friends more or less."

"Just think about it, okay? You know you're going nowhere this way."

Anvil got up and walked away, leaving Doug sitting there with little to do but watch the brailer bags as they hovered over containers to empty their loads of fish when a worker pulled the release cord at the bottom. By now his beard was pretty full and had surprisingly come in red, and with the bandana he always wore pirate style on his head, he was unrecognizable.

Why was his old friend Jeff so resistant to returning to a main-stream kind of life?

He had always been a productive kind of guy—almost to a fault. This new persona was completely out of character for him. Doug looked over and watched his friend pace like a caged animal. What was going on inside him?

Just then he saw a worker pull another brailer release, the load of fish begin to drop, and then a body.

He rubbed his eyes in disbelief, but the commotion around the dock told him that what he had seen had been real. Anvil had seen it, too, and was quickly moving in his direction, seeming to make sure that the security guard got a good look at him as he did.

"Move it!" he called to Doug, starting to run toward the bikes.

By the time both men reached their bikes they were panting like a couple of old men.

"Now we're gonna ride past the plant real slow," Anvil said.

"Won't that arouse suspicion?' Doug asked.

"That's the plan," Anvil answered.

Once they fired up the bikes the two did just as Anvil had ordered and rode slowly past the gate, prompting the security guard to walk toward them.

"Hope that ain't Stritch," Anvil called, before breaking into a sinister laugh revving his engine and roaring off with Doug right behind.

Chapter Sixty-One

Surrounded by the Law

"What are you doing, Jeff?" Doug demanded after they had pulled into a secluded spot down the road.

"Look, Doug, I know what I'm doing here. Now I'm gonna need you to do something to help me—something dangerous, but necessary, and I'm gonna make sure we've got your back."

"We?" Doug answered.

"Me and the rest of the FBI," Anvil said, flashing a badge. "I've been working undercover for a couple of years."

"You kidding me?" Doug answered. "Are you stinking kidding me?"

"You got a boat named the *Storm Roamer*? And another one named the *Driftfeather*? A wife named Mara—who escaped her security by the way—and a niece named Anna, who works for us? A deck-hand named Hamlet?"

"Holy almighty!" Doug said.

"How about your friend, Derrk Stanley, his son, Joey, his deckhand, Cory, and the other one named J.D.?"

Doug just stared.

"A mother-in-law named Sylvia/Sal, a father-in-law named Joe . . ."

"Okay, I get it," Doug said. "Cops everywhere but yet I'm always getting hung up in this kind of thing."

"Recognize the name, Carlos Antoya? Maybe if I tell you that he's involved, you'll listen to me," Anvil said.

Anvil proceeded to fill Doug in on the escape of Carlos Antoya and the infiltration of a string of drug runners from the cartel into Alaska.

"He's been running his operation from prison and now that he's escaped, we have reason to believe that he's now here," Anvil said.

"What's all this got to do with me and what do you need me to do?" Doug asked. "I mean, how did I end up with another cop? What are the odds?"

Anvil reached for Doug's jacket, took out a pocketknife, and made a slit through the threads that held an inner pocket closed. Then he pulled out a small metal object.

"GPS," he said.

"But how did you know I would go somewhere where there was a cop?"

Doug was genuinely perplexed. The thought of having this kind of intrusion into his very mindset frightened him.

"That was pure, unadulterated luck on our part," Anvil said. "And probably on yours, too, if you think about it."

"So you know everyone—Jocelyn Sanders? Stovepipe? Ted?"

"We're all in this together. This is major, Doug."

Doug revved his bike and sped off, spinning a few brodies, and then coming back.

"What about my boats?"

"Right now, Anna is on the *Storm Roamer* with Hamlet. They're hiding Mara there in a secret compartment they found in the hull. Derrk, Joey, Cory, and J.D. are on the *Driftfeather*, and they think they're hung up in Dutch for a Coast guard inspection issue."

"Can't stall things forever with that story," Doug said.

"The big issue, though, is that we believe that Carlos Antoya is right here in Dutch and that he's been smuggling in both members of the cartel and black tar heroin on fishing boats—possibly even yours."

"No way!" Doug said, jumping up.

"They're good, Doug. Skilled at what they do."

"I would have found some sign—" Doug said.

"Does the fact that Hamlet pulled a package of gray bandanas with orange volcanoes in the corners out of the secret compartment in the hull of the *Storm Roamer* surprise you?"

Doug stood, flabbergasted.

"Or the fact that the dead body that your wife found on the beach turned out to be a greenhorn that worked alongside Joey Stanley's friend, Cory, seem like too loose a connection to you?"

"And, Derrk? Is he a suspect, too?" Doug asked.

"I'm not going to comment on that just yet," Anvil replied. "But his son, Joey? Maybe. And, some of the others—definitely."

"As things stand right now, that security guard has got a dead body on his hands, and he's already had a couple of run-ins with a pair of no-good bikers looking for a guy named Stritch. When all this pans out, he'll decide that the body is Stritch, no matter what the guy's real name is—and then we'll wait."

Doug scratched his head and squinted at Anvil.

"Wait?"

"Yup. Wait. Since it looks like our intelligence about another murder coming down with this incoming load was right, and if it turns out our hunch about the rest of the players in this bust is right on, too, we're going to be hearing from Carlos Antoya real soon."

"Maybe sooner than you think, gringos." A voice behind them said.

Anvil whipped around and simultaneously pulled his gun, but not before Carlos Antoya dropped him with a barrage of gunfire from his assault rifle.

"Jeff!" Doug called as he dove for his friend.

"Much as I'd like to add another Williams bro to my list of successful kills," Carlos Antoya said, "I've got other plans for you, my friend."

Doug tried to reach for Jeff again, but was blocked by Carlos Antoya, who had now been joined by two other men.

"You can't help him, gringo. He's with his savior now."

And then Carlos Antoya began laughing in a way that sent chills down the spine of the currently red-bearded Doug Williams.

"I like what you've done to your face," Carlos sneered. "The red is a nice touch. Shave it!" he commanded, prompting his two men to step forward only to be blocked by their commander.

"Just kidding," Carlos laughed. "No seriously, you will need to shave it, my friend. I'm going to need you to get your boat, the *Driftfeather*, moved either somewhere away from the Coast guard station, or back out to sea."

"What do you need my seiner for?" Doug asked.

"I don't need your seiner, Williams, but I do need to remove about 2 million dollars worth of high-grade smack from the hull."

"Why do you think I'll help you?" Doug said.

"Maybe because I've got your wife and your niece locked up on the *Storm Roamer* and they're getting kind of tired of babysitting the corpse of the superagent they called Hamlet."

"You son-of-a—" Doug said, lunging forward.

"Now, now, my friend, don't get all testy now," Carlos said, grabbing Doug by the arm and twisting it to the near breaking point.

"Handcuff him, but don't leave any marks!" Carlos said in Spanish to his thugs.

Chapter Sixty-Two

Respect, of Sorts

With handcuffs firmly in place, Doug stopped resisting, letting Carlos's men take him back to a motel room in Unalaska. There, they patted him down and then sent him into the bathroom, where he was told to take a shower and shave.

"We want you looking like your normal self," Carlos said. "First thing you're going to do is to identify my head runner, who had the unfortunate mishap inside the brailer, as one of your greenhorns."

Doug wasn't sure who had killed the man that he and Anvil had dubbed Stritch, but obviously it was important to Carlos Antoya that he be legitimized, even in death.

When Doug undressed to climb into the shower, he was surprised to find a small piece of metal inside his shoe. He picked it up and realized that it was the GPS that Jeff had told him about. He heard the door rattle and made a snap decision to swallow it.

He wasn't sure how long it would stay inside his body, but the way things were going, he wouldn't be needing that much time anyway. He was convinced that either the rest of the FBI would find him, or he was living his final days on earth. Hopefully, somebody besides the two dead agents had been tracking him and would be showing up soon.

"Whaz taking you so long?" one of Carlos's men said, after spitting in the toilet.

"Need a razor," Doug answered.

"Yeah, right," the guard laughed. "Here," he said, throwing an old electric razor in Doug's direction. "Don't get any razor burn."

It was creepy, the way Carlos and his men were always laughing at everything—not that their braying attempts at humor could be construed as funny. No, their laughter was the depraved bleating spewed forth from the face of evil—chilling, callous, and hair-raising.

Doug walked out of the shower, plugged in the razor, and lifted it to his face as Carlos's thug stood sneering at him from the doorway.

"Get back out here, Moron!" Carlos called to the man who was leering at Doug.

Doug kept shaving as the thug backed away and shut the door. Outside he heard what sounded like someone shoving someone against the wall, a gunshot, and then silence.

When he stepped back out of the bathroom after finishing his shower, he saw the guard limping around the room, with a bloody rag tied around his thigh and the fear of god written across his face.

"Allow me to apologize for the rudeness of my guard," Carlos said. "And remind you that Carlos Antoya is the king of men and will not be disrespected by anyone, not even his own brother, right, Miguel?"

"Si," the man with the injured leg replied in Spanish. "My brother is the king of men."

"Come here, baby brother," Carlos called, cradling the grown man's head against his chest. Your 'king of men' brother will get you all fixed up now, okay?"

Chapter Sixty-Three

It's Going Down

Mara and Anna sat quietly in the galley of the *Storm Roamer,* under the watchful eye of three of Carlos's thugs.

"Throw it overboard," Carlos Antoya commanded, pointing to Hamlet's lifeless body.

As both women quietly sobbed, the thugs complied.

"Shut up!" Carlos Antoya shouted.

"C'mon, baby," they heard a female voice say from the doorway.

Carlos Antoya whipped around and backhanded the woman across the face, causing her to stumble forward and land at the feet of Mara and Anna.

"Della?" Mara gasped. "OMG! Della?"

"I said shut up," Carlos Antoya yelled.

Della began to vomit. Her skin was pale and sweaty and she was beginning to shake.

"Maybe you need old Carlos, huh?" Carlos said. "And maybe Carlos still needs you. Give it to her!"

Anna and Mara watched as one of Carlos's men handed Della a syringe, a spoon, a lighter, and a small bag holding a powdered substance. They watched as Della fumbled to empty the contents of the bag into the spoon, heat it with the lighter, then draw it into the syringe, but they both turned away when she pulled a tiny mirror out of her pocket and used it to guide the needle to a vein under her tongue, where she injected the substance despite the obvious pain the process was causing her.

Almost instantly they watched Della's color return, the sweating stop, and the pain disappear from her face.

"Sorry about the mess," she laughed, reaching for some paper towels to clean up the vomit.

"You'll excuse me, ladies," Carlos Antoya said.

Mara winced as he took Della by the arm that she had so painstakingly nursed back to productivity, and led her out of the seiner.

"I got a little surprise for you, Mrs. Williams," he said on the way out the door.

Just then two men walked in, pushing Doug ahead of them.

"Doug!"

But her husband did not break the look of intense concentration on his face.

"I want you to start up the seiner and start backing out of the harbor."

"But the Coast guard—"

"Do what I'm telling you, Mara."

"Anna, you pull anchor and provide backup."

Anna nodded.

"I'm going to be back just before you pull out," Doug said, "but first I have to talk to Derrk and his crew and find a way to make this okay with the Coast guard."

Doug knew full well that what was about to happen was not going to be okay with the Coast guard, but he needed Mara to stay calm.

"Whatever happens," he said, hoping that someone was picking up a signal from the GPS he had swallowed, "Keep pulling away—even if I don't make the jump . . ."

Mara and Anna both nodded.

While he had been talking, Carlos's thugs had been pacing outside the door.

"Hurry up, gringo," one of them called.

Doug began backing away, but not before mouthing the words he hoped and prayed Mara would be able to interpret: "Tell Coast guard, Pirates. Tell Coast guard, Pirates. Copy? Tell Coast guard, Pirates."

Mara squinted and used every ounce of fortitude she possessed to not show any expression on her face. If Doug had seen the slight glimmer of recognition in her eyes, he didn't show it either, but somehow, inside, he sensed that she had understood.

One of the thugs stayed behind as the other two left with Doug. She watched through the wheelhouse window as her husband signaled for Derrk to pull away in the *Driftfeather* and then walked into the Coast guard station.

Suddenly, spinning around he yelled, "Mara! Go! Go!" Then turning to the Coast guard officer on duty he yelled, "Pirates!"

Mara had already fired up the *Storm Roamer* and was slowly backing it out of the slip and turning it around when Carlos's man lunged for her only to be tackled by a fast-thinking Anna.

Thinking on her feet, Mara made a sudden sharp turn, causing Anna to roll on top of the guard. Out of the corner of her eye, she saw a struggle, heard a gunshot, and then another.

"Punch it, Mara!" Anna said, standing up.

Mara began moving the *Storm Roamer* away from the harbor to the sound of gunfire erupting behind them on the *Driftfeather*. All hell was breaking loose as the Coast guard and a swarm of men in blue descended on the seiner, *Driftfeather*. As police cars with lights and sirens came from seemingly out of nowhere, she heard Anna calling, "Uncle Doug, hurry! Hurry!"

But there was no way he was going to make it to the *Storm Roamer*. Was that Carlos Antoya with a couple of his men running after him?

"Uncle Doug! Dive! Dive!"

Mara shuddered in horror as she heard the sounds of an automatic rifle firing in their direction.

"Keep moving, Mara!"

But the *Storm Roamer* was unable to pick up enough speed and she could hear the sound of bullets hitting its sides.

"On the floor, Mara! Now!" Anna screamed, throwing herself down onto the deck, as Mara put the throttle in neutral.

For the next several minutes the two women lay on the floor as the *Storm Roamer* floated in the harbor, and the sound of automatic gunfire rang out in every direction.

Then she heard Anna again, "Doug! Doug!"

Unable to stay down any longer, Mara rose up just in time to see Anna stand at the back of the seiner, raise the gun she had taken from the dead guard, and fire two shots at something near the seiner.

Only when she saw Anna slowly sit down did she dare look over the side. There, lying dead inside a skiff, were Carlos Antoya and one of his men, with a quivering Della still alive.

Behind them, they could see police swarming the *Driftfeather*, followed by the removal of at least six men, who were being led off the seiner single file, each with his hands in the air. On the dock behind them, Doug stood up and waited with his hands in the air while police approached him.

Mara watched as they lowered his arms, and escorted him to safety. Only then did she help Anna throw a rope to the skiff so that they could pull Della behind them to shore.

Chapter Sixty-Four

Still Alive

Once back to shore, the *Storm Roamer* was met by Jocelyn Sanders and Barb, both of whom hugged Mara and Anna as they assisted them off the seiner.

Seeming to notice that Anna was particularly subdued, Jocelyn Sanders took her aside.

"He was a great agent and a great man—you know, Hamlet," Anna said.

"I know, dear," Jocelyn Sanders said, showing an uncharacteristic soft side.

"He didn't deserve—then I killed someone . . ." Anna broke into sobs.

"We've all been there. The first kill . . ." Jocelyn Sanders began.

"Uncle Doug!" Anna cried, running to Doug Williams.

"It's okay, Anna," Doug said. "I saw what happened. You were amazing! Calm. Steady. Brave."

"He was going to kill you and Mara," Anna said. "I had to do it. I didn't have a choice."

"He was evil, Anna. He killed my brother—your father. Then there's what he did to Della . . ."

Hard as it was, Mara held back in order to let Doug comfort Anna, then suddenly she ran to him, too. As the three of them stood there embracing, Jocelyn Sanders returned to the group followed by the greenhorn, J.D.

"Justin?" Mara exclaimed. "Justin Smith? You're alive?"

"I think so," he said, pinching his arm.

"We had to make it look like he was dead to put him under-cover," Barb said.

"So, it was no accident, then, that you were in the coffee shop?"

Barb nodded. "No accident."

"Anna, I'm going to need to take a statement from you and fill out some paperwork on the issue of the use of deadly force," Justin Smith said. "Then you'll be placed on leave for three days pending forensics evaluation, but I think you know already—I certainly do—that there won't be any problem. Matter of fact, I can't think of one person on this earth that won't be happy that Carlos Antoya is dead."

Escorted by Sergeant Justin Smith, Anna walked toward the main dock. The two slowed to allow the passage of Derrk Stanley and the deckhand, Cory, who were being moved to a patrol car.

Suddenly Cory lunged at Anna and Justin, spewing expletives as he did.

"Lucky break for you, copper," he said to Justin. "'Cause you were going to be the next dead body, but your friend, Hamlet, saw me in town and sent me back to the *Driftfeather*. And you . . ." he cursed at Anna. "Shoulda known a goody-two-shoes like you was a cop."

Justin Smith took a couple of steps toward Cory and then stepped back, taking Anna by the arm and walking around him as two police officers wrestled him into a squad car.

"You were quite the actress in convincing him that you loved him," Justin Smith told the still-quivering Anna. "Might have to put you in for an Academy Award."

Chapter Sixty-Five

More Questions than Answers

Doug and Mara Williams walked back and helped an officer bring Della up onto the dock from the skiff that still held the now deceased Carlos Antoya.

"Why, Della?" Mara asked.

Della looked dazed and avoided making eye contact as they assisted her out of the small boat.

"You have the right to remain silent . . ." an officer began.

Della looked up as if in a fog as the officer read her her rights.

"What's going to happen to her?" Mara asked Captain Sanders.

"Depends on her involvement in the drug distribution scheme they had going, but I suspect she was a victim herself," Captain Sanders replied. "I'm pretty anxious to talk to her."

"Can I talk to her?" Mara asked.

"I'm sorry, Mrs. Williams," Jocelyn Sanders answered, waving on the officer who was transporting Della.

"I'm going to need to call Joe," Mara told Doug.

Meanwhile, officers were in the process of moving Derrk Stanley into a patrol car.

For just a second, Derrk made eye contact with the man who had trusted him with everything he had, then he looked away.

Jocelyn Sanders walked up to Doug and Mara, silently accompanying them off the docks, where none other than Ben Donaley met them.

"It's over now," he said gently. "The death of Carlos Antoya brings an end to one of the longest-running cartels in South America."

"So that *was* you I saw at the garage," Doug said. "Did you know about Anna, too?"

"Larry Kenton and I go way back, Doug. We were rookies together at the academy. And as for Anna, well, I've been grooming her for this job ever since her mother and I got married."

"It's gonna be great to get rid of this stovepipe leg," Larry Allen Kenton said, walking up to the group.

"Well I know I'm getting kind of tired of hearing you complain about it every night," Jocelyn Sanders said. "Being married to an undercover agent is no danged picnic."

Doug and Mara both just stared. Virtually every person they had come in contact with since Mara had found the body on the beach in Homer had been a cop.

The biggest surprise, though, had been Ben Donaley, who both of them thought was long retired and holding down the homestead while his wife was visiting friends Outside.

"It was touch and go for a while—especially after Carlos Antoya killed Jeff," Ben Donaley said, "but you were smart, Doug, to keep that GPS chip on your person. Every cop in Dutch Harbor's been watching your every move since yesterday."

Doug sat down and Mara followed suit. This had all come down so fast. After literally months and months of anguish and uncertainty, it was hard to believe it was over.

What about the rest of the cartel? Would they seek revenge for the killing of Carlos Antoya? Why had they killed at least two young men—and tried to kill Doug? Why had Doug and Mara been targeted? Why Sal and Joe? What was Della's involvement?

How could they be sure it really was over this time?

Chapter Sixty-Six

Pieces to the Puzzle

Over the next couple of weeks, the answers to many of the questions started coming in. The saga tracked back to the time when Mara first came to Alaska and was tied, as it had been once before, to the activities of her first husband (and Ben Donaley's son), Brad.

Once the South American cartel had identified Dan Williams as the one person who had derailed their Alaska operation, it had targeted his entire family. Even over time, when things seem to have been resolved, they continued to surface in the lives of Doug and Mara due to one post-Brad, post-Dan common denominator, and that person was determined to be Derrk Stanley.

Derrk had worked diligently to gain the trust of Doug Williams, even working himself into the esteemed position of close friend. The truth of the matter, though, was that Derrk had been using Doug all along to rake in millions of dollars from the transport and sale of high-quality illegal drugs, as well as the smuggling in of key members of the cartel.

He had done so using the secret compartments in the twin seiners, *Storm Roamer and Driftfeather,* and all right under the nose of their owner, Doug Williams. As much as Doug Williams had practiced the hands-on approach to running his fishing operation, he had always relied on Derrk to go down into the hold for inspections and repairs—always, since day one.

He had also relied on Derrk to run early maintenance on the seiners after returns from trips out to sea or to other ports, usually returning the next day to assist with cleanup and repairs. All of this had made it easy enough for Derrk to smuggle both cartel members and contraband aboard the seiners, get them secured in the secret compartments and transported, all without detection.

The FBI had suspected Derrk for some time, but in order for them to gather enough evidence to successfully put him away for life, they needed to make him feel that he was above suspicion, thus his placement into the witness protection program.

Derrk had also taken command of the galley, thus keeping a safe distance between Doug, other crew members, and the fugitives who were breathing through a series of vents in the floor of the galley/roof of the secret compartments.

Although this arrangement usually worked, there had been a couple of times when things had taken a downturn with dire consequences, causing Derrk to have to find a way to dispose of the bodies of fugitives who did not survive the oppressive conditions in the hull compartment.

The first of these casualties had been the body that Mara had found washed up in Homer. Derrk had been proud of his plan to make the bodies appear to have died from more sinister causes, thus applying the ropes and bandanas to deflect suspicion away from the real reason for the demise of the unlucky thugs—all while feigning as much horror and surprise as everyone else.

Derrk had become so skillfully subversive, that he had even eventually dragged his own son, Joey into the fray, by pretending that Joey had gotten involved with the smugglers.

When Della had seen him handing a bag of contraband over the rail of the *Driftfeather,* Derrk had threatened to tell Joe Michael the real reason why his feather had turned up missing: that after her mother died, Della had been trying to rent it to hapless victims who hoped to benefit from its supposed magical protective powers, and using that money to support the heroin habit she had developed after first becoming addicted to her dying mother's pain pills.

Delbert Green, a.k.a. Hamlet, had once approached Derrk with his suspicions about Della, prompting Derrk to hold the older deck hand at arm's length and getting him reassigned from the *Driftfeather* to the *Storm Roamer*.

"The guy creeps me out," Derrk had once told Doug. "Acts like a narc or something, I don't know . . ."

Even though Doug had assured Derrk that Hamlet was no more than a crusty old seasoned deckhand, Derrk had insisted that he be kept off the *Driftfeather*.

As Carlos Antoya began to grow more demanding about the amount of contraband and speed with which Derrk was operating, Derrk had lured Della into a connubial relationship with the drug kingpin, despite the fact that the drug lord was already married to a woman in Peru.

The relationship served two purposes: to satisfy the insatiable and lewd carnal appetite of Carlos Antoya, and to provide Della with all the heroin she needed and wanted to support her habit without her having to take to the streets.

The fact that Della had gone from being the sweet and loyal person everyone loved to a conniving junkie had meant nothing to Carlos Antoya, who was already in the process of finding a way to get rid of her and take on a new love interest that he had met along the way.

Della's position in Carlos Antoya's hierarchy had become so precarious, in fact, that had the siege on the *Storm Roamer* and the *Driftfeather* not happened when it did, her body would have been the next one to float to shore with a gray bandana bearing an orange volcano symbol in the corner tied to it.

As things had played out though, she had been spared, but to what extent and for how long remained unknown. Her knowledge of and involvement in drug running was not going to work in her favor, no matter how convincing the argument was that she herself had been a victim of the evil drug lord. And her heavy addiction to heroin had become problematic enough that it was doubtful that she would now be able to afford to support her habit—a reality that would likely drive her to the streets if she was lucky enough to escape jail time.

"It's a complicated and convoluted sequence of major international crime," Ben Donaley said to Doug and Mara over breakfast one morning. "And it's going to take years to further piece it all together if doing so at this point is even possible at all."

On seeing the worry on Mara's face, he added, "But Carlos Antoya is dead and we have a clearly established link to his determination to terrorize the lives of you and Doug and anyone and everyone close to you. For that be thankful, because as horrific as all of this was, it's over now, and no matter how many years it remains a burning hole in the minds of law enforcement, at long last—finally—you and Doug and all of us you love are free. We are all really and truly free."

Chapter Sixty-Seven

Be It Resolved . . .

B y the time Mara and Doug got to Sitka, Derrk Stanley had been arraigned on multiple federal and state charges regarding the transport and sale of controlled substances, smuggling, kidnapping, hijacking, murder, attempted murder, and a host of other charges. He had been denied bail because of being an international flight risk, and was currently being housed in a maximum-security section of an undisclosed Alaska prison.

His son Joey had also been arraigned, although authorities were in the process of attempting to grant him immunity in exchange for his testimony.

The fate of Della had been less straightforward. Although it had been Joe Michael's desire to go to her and try to help, authorities had convinced him that the effort would be futile.

Still, because of the anxiety and disarray in the lives of Joe, Sal, Doug, and Mara, the totem ceremony was delayed until the final resolution of the activities and players in the crime organization could be determined.

During multiple interviews with Della, authorities gathered considerable evidence linking the activities of Derrk Stanley to those of Carlos Antoya and his cartel—testimony that completely exonerated

Doug, Mara, Sal, and Joe Michael from any illegal involvement in the illicit operations.

Authorities had worked quickly to bring the case to trial and within the span of six months, Derrk Stanley had been sent to federal prison for 369 years. His son, Joey, had fared better, receiving only one sentence of five years for his part in collusion, although the extenuating circumstances wrought by the control of his father had prompted the judge to waive four of those years if Joey showed good behavior and enrolled in some type of academic program toward a goal of self-sufficiency in life.

During this time, in lieu of prison, and on the recommendation of Jocelyn Sanders and Joe and Sal Michael, Della had been enrolled in an intensive, high-security rehabilitation facility for no less than six months, where by all accounts, she was making excellent progress in conquering her severe and longtime addiction to heroin.

All the members of her extended family had been steadfast in their willingness to help Della succeed in conquering her addiction, and had rotated visits with the young woman to ensure that she had ongoing and consistent support as she worked toward recovery.

The many other members of Carlos Antoya's cartel, who had been busted during the storming of the *Driftfeather* were now facing their own trials, and many of them deportation, especially after two more bodies had been discovered in the islands near Dutch Harbor, Alaska.

Not only had the cartel and near empire of Carlos Antoya been dealt a fatal blow, it had been permanently dismantled with the cooperation of South American authorities, who had shut down and destroyed his compound in Peru and permanently lowered and destroyed the cartel's flag, which was of a gray fabric with white bandana-style markings and an orange volcano in one corner.

Along with being one of the most vicious cartel leaders in the world of drugs and smuggling, Carlos Antoya had enjoyed the dubious distinction of being universally hated even by other drug kingpins—not necessarily unusual in the underworld, but distinctive in that they bore no respect for the level of cruelty and depravity that he exercised in the running of his operation.

As hard as it was for law enforcement to grasp that there was "honor among thieves," there was no denying that a hierarchy of leadership and a code of conduct existed even among the world's most desperate criminals and Carlos Antoya had failed to gain even a modicum of acceptance within that world.

The result of this disaffection for Carlos Antoya and his cartel had been that no other group would allow assimilation of any portion of his now greatly weakened organization to infiltrate into their own. In fact, in a highly unusual move, several cartel leaders had publicly expressed their disdain for both Carlos Antoya and all that he stood for, and had also pledged to annihilate any remnants of his operation they might become aware of, including killing members of his former team.

Carlos Antoya, his cartel, and the very legend of his existence were dead and had been relegated to a buried piece of history that no one now alive would ever honor with any type of active or passive continuation within their own organizations either now or in the future.

Joe Michael's words to Mara Benson Edwards Williams Benson Williams had indeed been prophetic:

YOUR PRESENT IS THE FUTURE OF YOUR PAST
YOU WILL NEED THIS TO PROTECT YOUR FUTURE FROM YOUR PAST
ALL WHO COME HERE SEEK THE FUTURE OF THEIR PAST

With the demise of the South American cartel led by this evil man, Mara's past had been reconciled, never to control her or the lives of those she loved again.

It was a knowledge that she had not yet been able to grasp as the haunting recollections of the last several years in Alaska played out in her mind. She and Doug had decisions to make in the coming months—decisions about whether they would stay in their adopted state and continue to embrace its incredible goodness and beauty, or whether they would choose to make a clean break and move somewhere else.

Although all bets were on them remaining in the Land of the Last Frontier, even they could not be sure, but the point was that they were free now. Free to be who they were always meant to be, and free to pursue their happiness without fear, and that freedom alone marked the beginning of the rest of their lives.

Chapter Sixty-Eight

Resolution

The day of the pole-raising ceremony was bittersweet. With a light rain falling over Sitka, Mara, Doug, and Sal made their way to the site that had been chosen for the totem.

Joe Michael had gone to the place earlier and was standing with his friend, John, and John's son when the three approached him. A few minutes later, Della arrived, looking fresh and more alive than she had been in years.

Joe Michael embraced her, whispering that he had something he wanted to talk to her about after the ceremony. Then, one by one, he embraced Mara, Doug, and lastly, his dear wife, Sal.

He and Sal had already begun rebuilding their home in Hoonah, choosing a site closer to the water, where the salvage operation had once taken place. Their old home site would house a new hangar and a new shop, with plenty of room for a cabin if Doug and Mara decided they wanted one—and space for Della, too, although she had told them she was moving in another direction.

Joe Michael fingered the feather in his pocket before removing it and handing it to Della.

"I want you to have this," he told her. "And Mara does, too."

Della took the feather and placed it in her pocket, turning her head to hide any emotion she felt, while Joe and the others gathered around the pole.

They stood silently as John walked up one side of the totem and down the other, holding a cedar branch over it as he moved. They bowed their heads as he spoke in Tlingit, then in Haida, asking for it to be blessed by the Creator. Then he asked the Creator to protect those gathered around it before laying the cedar branches on the ground and lighting them on fire.

The warmth of the flames felt welcoming in the cold rain, as the branches flared, smoked, and then simmered in a gentle fire from which two larger branches that had been placed under them were removed and held alongside the bottom of the pole until the entire rounded end of it had been charred.

Those present knew the significance of the charring, and that it sealed in a protective layer between the totem and the earth, allowing it's message to rise upward toward the sky.

A pair of eagles had built a nest nearby, and so with great care, a dozen strong men raised the pole, using a series of ropes tied about a third of the way from the top, and a series of wooden braces to assist with the process.

Both Joe Michael, John, and John's son, as carvers, assisted the process, with each of them holding a ceremonial rope. Alongside the pole, a shaman wearing traditional garb, prayed. Mara stayed back and took as many pictures as she could of the event.

At the end of the ceremony, as the crowd gathered around the totem, there was widespread speculation about the significance of the eagles, their nest and their flight from the nest just as the pole was centered in its hole. A few old-timers even questioned the absence of ravens, wondering if that foretold the coming of a significant change.

"The eagle is the raven is the eagle," one man said. "And the flight of the eagles is a signal for the ravens to return."

As smoke from the burning cedar branches wafted skyward, Joe Michael walked to the totem and placed his hand squarely on the red dot he had carved there, not once, but twice. He was sure he felt it vibrate under his hand—or was the sensation all the emotion he was feeling inside? Whatever the case, he held his hand there and felt the warmth flow from his body into the totem, seeking to energize it with his own aura of love and hope and respect for his place before it.

When he removed his hand, the red dot glowed brightly, but then began to fade, taking on the more neutral hue of the reds found within the earth—like the very color he had mixed himself for the paint.

They did not tell him till later, and only after the lights and sirens of the ambulance had pierced the rain, that they had found Della in the woods near the place where Joe had hidden the paint cans, with a needle stuck in her arm, and the feather lying in her open hand.

Beside her, Joe's can of red paint lay open, and beside it, written on a fallen log the words: I HAVE ALWAYS LOVED YOU ALL.

In large part because of the note, Della's recently uplifted behavior, and her years of distress and abuse, the coroner deemed her death a suicide by overdose of heroin—a fact that was substantiated later by toxicology tests that ruled out foul play.

"I never got to tell her," Joe Michael told Sal.

"She knew you loved her," Sal answered. "And at long last she is at peace."

Doug and Mara watched as Joe and Sal walked away hand in hand. In a week they would return and scatter Della's ashes under the totem, after the proper paperwork had been completed.

"It's time for us to start living," they heard him tell Sal. "The circle of my past is now closed and a new present and future can begin."

The significance of the rainbow that appeared over Sitka Sound the day that Della's ashes were buried, was lost on no one, especially not on those who had loved her and walked the earth with the loving person she had always wanted to be.

Her demons notwithstanding, Della had left a huge mark on them all, one they would carry with fondness for the good times and joy that she had finally found peace.

Chapter Sixty-Nine

New Beginning

It was on a summer day up at Ellie and Ben's place on Knik River Road in Palmer that Anna and Justin Smith announced their engagement. Even Thor seemed to understand the miracle that had taken place in their coming together as a couple.

It was almost as if all the tragedy had kindled the spirit of strength that was this place where the two now chose to announce their love. All of it—Anna's father's death, the long road to healing from crossing paths with so many affected by that tragedy, the subsequent joy at seeing her father's homestead thrive in the hands of her mother's new husband, Ben Donaley, the coming together of Mara and Doug, Sarah and Ken, and even the saga with Sassy and her daughter, Erin—all of it.

Of course it would be a big wedding, in the tradition of that of which she had always dreamed. And they would all be there. All of them who had touched their lives in a good way, even if for some it would be only in spirit.

Anna knew that Dan would be pleased and on that summer solstice day, when Ben Donaley on one side and her mother on the other side walked her down the shore of the river, she felt her father's arms around her as if the gentle wings of an angel held her as she walked.

Thor was there, too, and wearing a collar made from flowers woven together by Anna herself. They matched the ring of flowers she wore on her head, and similar wristbands worn by her mother, Mara, and all the women close to her who were there.

Behind her, her Uncle Doug followed, assuming his role of protector for always having her back.

Justin Smith could barely contain his smile. Never had he imagined finding someone as sweet and as tough as Anna. As he stood on a large flat rock in the river, with a place beside him for his bride, Jocelyn Sanders and Larry Allen Kenton held hands.

Anna had not only planned a beautiful wedding, but she had planned a special series of ceremonies to follow. One by one, each of the couples in her and Justin's lives would renew their own vows and then they would celebrate as each began anew.

But for now the moment was about Anna and Justin. As they stood there in the sun, on a rock in the gently flowing river, they pledged their lives to each other as one by one their guests tossed flowers picked from Sassy's garden—enough to fill a horse watering trough that had been trucked over from her memorial garden—into the swiftly flowing current.

By all accounts, the ceremony had been as beautiful as any that had gone before, and when a flock of sandhill cranes flew by the bluff alongside Ben and Ellie's estate Anna and Justin stood together as husband and wife, alongside their family in a gathering of everything that represented the goodness in life.

"Let's dance!" Doug Williams shouted as he grabbed Mara around the waist and the band began to play. "Let's dance around Anna and Justin and let's dance for pure and simple joy."

The Beginning

Books Written By
Marianne Schlegelmilch

Solo Flite
An Alaska Puppy Becomes a Legend

Coho Waterboy
The Flat-Footed, Web-Footed Alaska Sled Dog

Raven's Light
A Tale of Alaska's White Raven

Gaston's Crow's Nest
An Alaska Tale

Feather From A Stranger
An Alaskan Mystery

Two Tickets and A Feather
Present Alaska--Future of her Past another Alaskan Mystery

Driftfeather on the Alaska Seas
Ultimate Future of the Past another Alaskan Mystery

Feather for Hoonah Joe
Alaska Can Be a Very Small Place

Feather for Forever
Alaska